HECK'S JOURNEY

A FRONTIER WESTERN

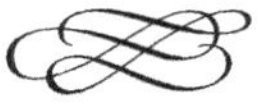

JOHN DEACON

Cover design by Angie on Fiverr

Edited by Karen Bennett

Want to know when my next book is released? SIGN UP HERE.

❀ Created with Vellum

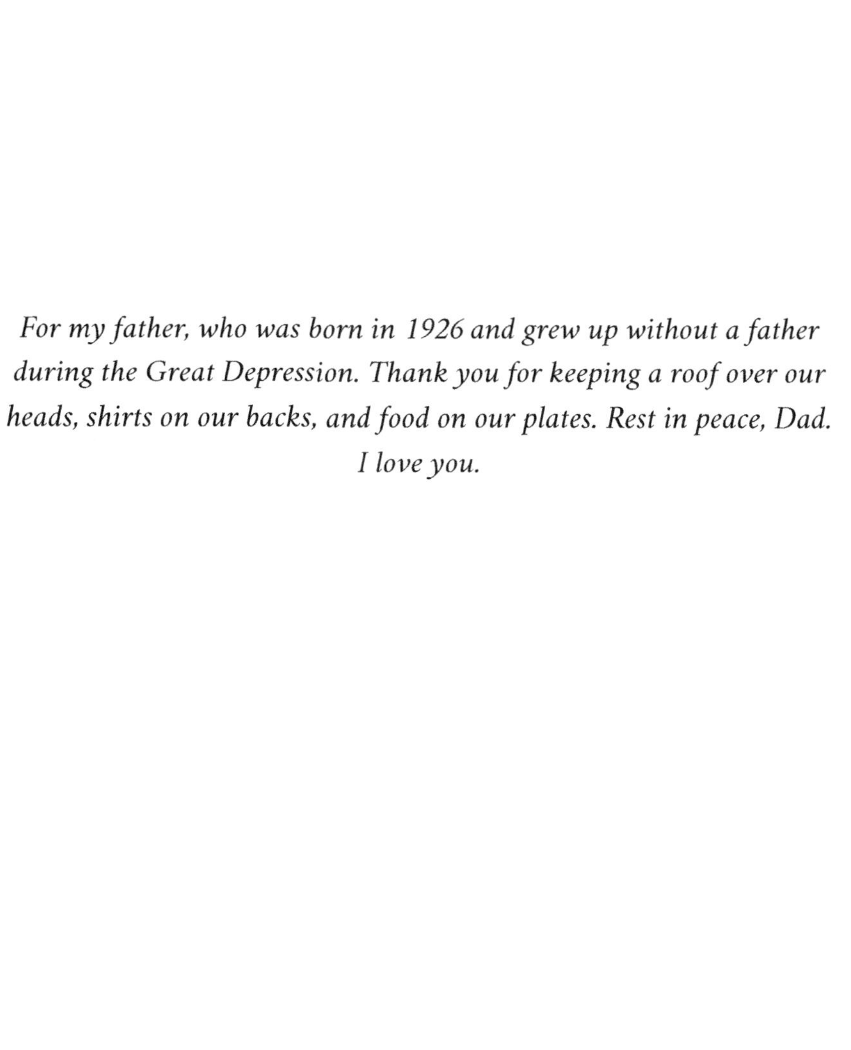

For my father, who was born in 1926 and grew up without a father during the Great Depression. Thank you for keeping a roof over our heads, shirts on our backs, and food on our plates. Rest in peace, Dad. I love you.

CHAPTER 1

Hector "Heck" Martin finished hammering the cross into the ground then crouched and ran his fingers over the name he'd etched into the plank, which until recently had been part of the small cabin he'd shared with Pa.

Hector Martin, Sr.
Beloved Father
1811 - 1847

"Lingering won't bring him back, boy," Mr. Detwiler said from atop the swayback dun. "Let's go."

"Yes, sir." Heck held back the tears and stood to his full height.

"You sure you're only fourteen?" Detwiler asked.

"Yes, sir."

"How'd you get so tall?"

"I don't know, sir. My grandpappy on my mother's side, I guess. I hear he was several inches over six feet."

"Well, being tall don't get you any extra to eat. You gotta earn every bite, boy. Your pappy asked me to look after you. Said he wanted you to go with me. Said you would work hard, earn your keep, and do everything I told you. Understand?"

"Yes, sir."

Heck picked up his haversack. There wasn't much in it.

He felt like he was in a daze. Just a few hours earlier, Detwiler had shown up with Pa tied across his horse and told how he'd gotten killed in a fight down by the river.

Then, while Heck set to digging the grave, Detwiler had ridden into town, sold Pa's few possessions, and come back smelling like whiskey.

All Heck had left in the world was a pocketknife, the clothes on his back, and his two prize possessions: Mother's old Bible and her wedding band, which he hid on a leather cord around his neck.

Heck couldn't remember Mother well. Cholera took her when he was four years old. But he remembered how she made him feel—like he was filled to the bursting with sunshine—and that was enough.

Now, Pa was gone, too. Heck had no siblings, no grandparents, no aunts, no uncles, nobody.

He was alone in the world.

"You know what indentured servitude is, boy?" Detwiler asked.

"Yes, sir." Heck's own ancestors had been kidnapped in

Ireland, sent to America, and put to work on plantations alongside African slaves.

"Well, that's your situation. That's how me and your pa set it up, see? He said if I would be so kind as to take care of you, you'd have to serve me for seven years."

LEAVING THE HOLLER, THEY MOVED STEADILY WEST. HECK walked behind Detwiler, who rode the dun. They worked wherever they could, though truth be told, Heck did all the working.

Detwiler's dishonesty was shocking to Heck. The man lied to everyone they met, telling them Heck was his son and saying that his wife, Heck's dear mother, had just passed on, and they were trying to work their way back to her parents' farm in Missouri to deliver the sad news.

Drinking at night around the campfire, Detwiler would recount the farmers' kindness with sneering laughter. "Did you see the woman start crying? The whole world's full of fools, boy, and you mountaineers are the biggest fools of all."

Heck said nothing to that and just kept leafing through the Bible, savoring every chapter, verse, and word and finding solace in the fact that his mother had turned these same pages and read these same words. Sometimes, he would also reread the names and dates of marriages and births Mother and her ancestors had recorded in the old book.

"All that Bible reading's gonna make you blind," Detwiler said. The man despised books the way some illiterate folks do, but even scoundrels like Detwiler respected the good book.

Otherwise, Detwiler would insist on selling the Bible. And that Heck would not do, no matter how much Detwiler cursed or beat him.

Detwiler used a thick hickory switch to beat the old mare and Heck alike, especially when Detwiler got to drinking.

Heck never let his pain show. His pa had taught him to respect his elders, so he didn't haul off and punch Detwiler, but he also wouldn't give him the satisfaction of wincing or crying out when the blows landed.

Days stretched into weeks. Heck walked behind Detwiler's horse, worked hard, and took his beatings without complaint. He rarely uttered a single word, just silently doing whatever Detwiler told him to do.

Except stealing.

On a few occasions while skirting the edge of some farm where plump chickens waddled in plain view, Detwiler would tell Heck to go steal them some dinner.

Heck refused. "My pa didn't raise me to be a thief."

On these occasions, Detwiler beat him more severely than ever, but Heck never caved.

Heck was hungry all the time. Detwiler worked him like a mule, and he'd walked all these miles with very little food.

Work wasn't hard to find, it being spring. But when they came into money, Detwiler favored whiskey over food. And when farmers paid in food, Detwiler took the lion's share.

Heck wished Detwiler hadn't sold his father's Kentucky rifle. With that old muzzleloader, Heck could part a squirrel's hair from 100 yards.

Meanwhile, Detwiler's flintlock pistol was no good for hunting whatsoever.

So Heck trudged hungrily on, determined to serve his seven years then strike off on his own and make a life for himself—likely in the West, where Pa had told him folks were staking new claims on the frontier and starting over.

Heck had to question the arrangement Pa had struck with Detwiler.

Why would a fiercely independent mountaineer like Pa set up a deal enslaving Heck for several years?

Whatever the case, Heck wouldn't dishonor the family name by cutting and running.

He'd do his time then make the most of his freedom in the West.

But despite Heck's determination, his plans came crashing down one night as they made a late camp on the banks of a river flanked by overhanging trees.

CHAPTER 2

Heck had worked for two days straight, putting up hay. His arms itched and burned, crosshatched in little scratches.

His stomach growled in anticipation of the pork and beans they were set to fry up.

Detwiler was even more cross than usual because he was out of whiskey. "Go take care of the horse, boy. I'll get a fire started."

Heck said nothing, but he was surprised. Building the night's fire was one of the many jobs Detwiler normally refused to do.

It would be nice to have a night off from gathering tinder and firewood. Unless, of course, Detwiler botched the job. In that case, he'd take it out on Heck. Some men were that way.

Heck took the dun down the bank to the water and let her drink her fill then led her over to a thick patch of grass and let her forage as he rubbed her down, talking softly to her since he knew Detwiler was out of earshot.

"You like that, Annabelle?" he asked, using the secret name he'd given her.

The mare lifted her head and brought her neck around to nuzzle him.

"That's a good girl, Annabelle." He hugged her. "I'll be back later, okay?"

Then, with his stomach growling louder than ever, he left her and went back up the embankment, where dark smoke was rising from their campsite.

Heck wasn't sure why, but that dark smoke put him on edge. It looked and smelled different than the smoke from the twigs, leaves, and dried grasses he gathered as kindling each night.

Then he heard Detwiler laughing.

The sound filled Heck with dread, because Detwiler only laughed at the expense of others.

Topping the rise, Heck stared in shocked disbelief. "What are you doing?"

Detwiler howled with laughter.

Heck rushed forward, burning his hands as he dragged his mother's Bible from the flames, beating at the charred pages, wanting to save them but knowing he was too late. The fire had destroyed not only God's word but also the handwritten chronicle of marriages and births, Heck's whole family tree.

Detwiler roared with amusement. "Well, boy, that good book sure does make good kindling!"

Heck leapt to his feet. His big, calloused hands balled into fists. "Why did you do that?"

"What? You expected me to go gather kindling? You should

thank me, boy. I saved you from all that reading. I'm telling you, someday you woulda—hey now, boy, you stay right where you are."

Heck kept marching toward him. For weeks, Detwiler had been working him, starving him, cussing him, and beating him, tamping down Heck's anger like gunpowder in a musket.

Detwiler's cruelty had finally sparked that powder.

The man stumbled backward, telling Heck to stop, a look of fear coming onto his face.

Somehow, this made Heck even angrier.

Detwiler panicked and sprinted off into the trees.

Heck plodded after him, fists swinging at his sides.

When Heck was fifteen feet from the trees, Detwiler stepped back into the open, pointing his pistol at him. "Now you stop, boy. You take another step, I'll blow you to Kingdom Come!"

Heck heard the hammer click into firing position but kept going as an icy calm settled over him.

Detwiler staggered backward, yodeling, "All right, boy! I'm gonna kill ya!"

Time slowed for Heck. With exquisite clarity, he saw Detwiler's hand wobble as the terrified man pulled the trigger.

Heck lurched to one side.

The gunshot boomed, and a line of fire burned across Heck's shoulder.

Then he was on him.

Every mountain boy learns to fight before he can even walk.

Heck clouted Detwiler with a powerful combination, smashing his big fists into the man's ears and jaw and nose and sending him reeling.

Heck reached out with his left, seized the barrel of the flintlock, and twisted with all his might, breaking Detwiler's finger and wrenching the weapon free as the man fell to the ground, dazed and whimpering.

Heck shoved the pistol through his belt, pulled his pocketknife, and snapped open the blade. His shoulder burned where the bullet had grazed him. "You shot me."

Detwiler struggled to his knees, weeping. "I didn't mean to. I was scared was all."

"You tried to kill me," Heck said. His hands were steady.

"No. I just wanted to scare you was all."

"I should kill you."

"Don't," Detwiler begged. "Have mercy, boy. I never meant—"

"Tell me the truth about my pa, and I'll let you live."

"Okay, boy. Your pa—"

Heck lowered the blade. "Careful, Detwiler. You don't tell me the truth, I'll slash your lying throat."

"Okay, okay," the man said. "I came upon your pa just after he was killed. All right? Some of the men asked did he have a family, and someone said yeah, he had a boy up in the holler, and they said they had to get him up there and tell the boy and all, and since I was the only one who had a horse..."

"So you lied about the rest of it."

"Don't kill me, boy. You promised. I told you the truth."

"Keep telling it, then. You lied, didn't you? You never talked to my pa."

Detwiler shook his head. "He was already gone before I got there."

Heck nodded. He had supposed as much for a long time, but

now, knowing he could walk away from this man without dishonoring his father, he felt incredibly free.

He went over to Detwiler's saddle bags and looked for anything of Pa's but found only Pa's money pouch, which had held a little over two dollars, but now held a half dime and two pennies.

Detwiler had drunk the rest.

Pa had worked hard to save that money. And Detwiler had wasted it with no more qualms than a fat woodchuck decimating a vegetable patch.

Heck was tempted to take the rest of Detwiler's gear, too, including the saddle bags, but he wouldn't stoop to Detwiler's level. Pa always said to beware low company because sooner or later they would drag you into a rut.

Heck reckoned he had good claim on the gun Detwiler had shot him with, and he refused to leave Annabelle there for him to beat, but Heck knew if he took the rest of the man's kit, he'd be sliding one foot down into that rut Pa mentioned.

Now that the fight was over, the gunshot started to throb. It was bleeding, too.

"I'm going," Heck said. "I'm taking Annabelle with me."

Detwiler looked at him like he was crazy. "Who's Annabelle?"

"The horse."

"Don't take my horse, boy. I can't walk all that way."

"I'm taking her. I won't let you keep beating her. I'm taking the pistol, too, along with the shot and powder. I'll leave the rest with you. It's more than you deserve."

"All right, boy. All right. Just go, then." Now that the man saw he would survive, anger built in him again. "You go ahead. Rob me blind and leave me all alone, you ungrateful whelp."

Heck stopped the man's tirade with an icy gaze. "One more thing, Detwiler. Don't get worked up and think you can come after me. I see you again, I'll kill you."

CHAPTER 3

As Heck traveled across Kentucky, folks surprised him with their warmth and hospitality. Farmers hailed him from their fields and invited him to dinner or supper or sometimes both.

Seeing his youth, they were interested in Heck's story and took pity, offering him a place to sleep and a stable and feed for Annabelle.

Early on, an elderly woman treated his gunshot wound, which was healing nicely. Most times, folks sent him off with a bit of food for the trail, too.

In return, Heck worked. Occasionally, he spent a few days with families who needed help. Spring was a busy time. These folks gave him other much needed gifts, including a rain slicker, a bedroll, a hatchet, and an iron skillet.

One farmer, marveling at Heck's hard work, offered him a permanent home.

"Thank you very much, sir," Heck responded, "but I reckon my heart's set on seeing the West."

Spring rains fell. Heck rode through showers, taking his time and minding the trail. When heavy rains pounded down, he holed up, mostly under pines.

He was hungry all the time.

Hungry but happy. Yes, he missed Pa, but if he built his new life around mourning the lost, he'd have no better future than a droopy mushroom growing on a mossy log.

Instead, he pointed himself toward a brighter future. He was young and strong and determined, and he believed in the West and the life he could build in it.

When the weather broke, he followed a creek out of the woods and into a stretch of lush farm country.

There were more houses here, more roads, more people, and he knew he was getting closer to a town, though he couldn't have guessed what town. He didn't even know if he was in Kentucky anymore.

His stomach growled constantly. He was scanning the territory, looking for a farmer who might need a hand, when he spotted the buggy stuck in the creek.

The driver, a boy older but smaller than Heck, struggled mightily, trying to get the horse and buggy out of the muddy creek.

On the bank, two other boys of sixteen or seventeen years hooted with laughter, doing nothing to help and ridiculing the driver, whom they called Tom.

Red-faced, Tom struggled hopelessly.

Meanwhile, two women sat in the buggy, watching Tom with horrified expressions.

Heck rode over, dismounted, and hitched Annabelle to an elm. Then he waded into the creek. He nodded at Tom and approached the buggy, where he spoke to the woman who seemed to be Tom's mother.

"Ma'am," Heck said, "if you'll allow me to help you ladies to dry ground, I reckon your son and I can take care of this."

"Thank you, young man," the woman said.

Heck carried her in his arms across the powerful stream and deposited her on dry ground.

The boys on the opposite shore laughed like they'd never seen anything so funny.

Heck waded back to the buggy.

"Thanks for your help," Tom said with a worried expression and held out his hand.

"Glad I came by when I did. We'll get you back on the road in no time."

"Well, I appreciate it. I'm Tom Mullen."

"Heck Martin. Good to meet you."

He went back around the buggy, and the other woman moved forward. As Heck really saw her for the first time, his heart lurched to a stop, freezing him for an instant. In that moment, he couldn't feel the cold water, couldn't hear the obnoxious laughter of the boys on the other bank, couldn't perceive anything except the vision of utter loveliness smiling down at him from the buggy seat.

She was not a woman, he realized, but a girl, a girl around his age, and the prettiest thing he had ever seen by a far stretch. Thick auburn locks framed her heart-shaped face, which shone with health and humor and happiness. Above a wide, bright white smile, green eyes stared at him, glittering as brightly as dew sparkling atop spring moss.

"Well, I sure am glad to see you, sir," she said. "Thank you so much for coming to our assistance."

For a second, Heck just stared at her. Never in his life had he seen anything half so lovely.

The girl laughed. It was a pretty sound he'd happily pay to hear again. "I'm Hope."

Heck blinked at her again. Then, realizing he was making a fool of himself, he smiled, his cheeks going hot. "Nice to meet you, ma'am. I'm Heck."

"Heck?" the girl laughed. "Are you teasing me? What sort of name is Heck?"

"It's short for Hector."

"Well, Heck, I am so grateful for your assistance. Now, are you going to help me out of this thing, or are you going to let me get swept away?"

"I will never let any harm come to you." Heck held out his arms, and Hope climbed into them.

Holding her was awkward but thrilling, and Heck wished the moment would never end, even though he felt painfully embarrassed by his tight and shoddy clothing and dirty face.

Smiling up at him with those sparkling eyes, Hope didn't seem to care if his face was dirty. Shockingly, she seemed to be enjoying the moment, too.

Heck moved slowly through the raging creek, careful to keep Hope's long dress from touching the water.

"Is it hard to carry me through this water?" she asked.

"No, ma'am. You're lighter than a newborn kitten."

Hope laughed at that. "Well, you must be very strong, Heck. And you sure are tall."

"Yeah, I've always been tall," he said, and then blushed again. That had been a stupid thing to say. But Hope was so pretty that he couldn't seem to think straight.

He placed her gently on dry ground, where Mrs. Mullen nodded approvingly.

Heck went back out, got behind the buggy, and put his shoulder into it, while Tom coaxed the horse.

The horse resisted until, with mighty effort, Heck started the wheels moving, and the buggy bumped into the horse's hindquarters. Seconds later, the buggy was up the bank and onto the road.

The whole time, the boys on the other shore hooted and catcalled, stirring fire in Heck's chest.

The Mullens started to thank Heck, but his work wasn't done yet. He begged their pardon and marched back into the creek.

The boys on the other side were older than him but must have recognized something dangerous in his expression, because they quit laughing and stared like a couple of scared rabbits at Heck, who stopped midstream and lifted a big hand to point back and forth between them.

"Why didn't you help these folks?" Heck demanded.

The boys muttered, dropping their eyes with obvious fear and embarrassment.

"You should've helped," Heck told them. "Now get out of here, or I'll thrash you both."

Without a word, the two boys leapt to their feet and ran off in the opposite direction.

When Heck went back across the stream, Hope was staring at him with a smile that stirred a different kind of fire in his chest.

Tom grinned after the fleeing boys. "Look at them run!"

A smiling Mrs. Mullen thanked Heck again. "I don't recognize you, young man. Who are your parents?"

"My parents have gone home to the Lord, ma'am."

"I am very sorry to hear that," Mrs. Mullen said. "With whom are you staying?"

Heck shook his head. "No one, ma'am. I'm just passing through."

"Well then, I insist that you come to our farm for supper. We have a spare bed and a warm, dry place for your horse."

CHAPTER 4

"And then Heck told them if they didn't get out of there, he was gonna whup 'em both," Tom laughed, ladling more gravy onto his potatoes.

Mr. Mullen leaned over and patted Heck's shoulder. The man had a pleasant face with a crooked nose and deep smile lines. He still spoke with a faint brogue, his own parents having come over from the Emerald Isle. "That's showing them, lad."

"Actually," Hope said, giving Heck a pretty smile, "what Heck said was, 'Why didn't you help these folks? You should've helped. Now get out of here or I'll thrash you both.'"

Heck was impressed that Hope had remembered everything he'd said, word for word.

Mr. Mullen laughed again. "Well, you're surely welcome at our table, Heck, and I'm very pleased to meet you."

"Thank you, sir," Heck said.

"Please hand me your plate, Heck," Mrs. Mullen said, "so I can fill it again."

Heck smiled at her. Inside he was torn. As usual, he was hungry, and he had never tasted such a delicious meal; but he didn't want to make a pig of himself.

"Thank you, ma'am, but I'm okay."

"Nonsense," Mr. Mullen said, grabbing Heck's plate and handing it to his smiling wife. "If you don't have more, Mrs. Mullen will take it to mean you don't appreciate her cooking."

Heck frowned at that. "That's not it at all, ma'am," he told Mrs. Mullen. "This is the best food I've ever tasted."

Clearly pleased, Mrs. Mullen loaded his plate with roasted chicken, beans, mashed potatoes, and gravy. "Thank you for the compliment, Heck. Don't be shy now. Eat your fill. But do save room for pie."

"I'll bet Heck could eat ten plates," Hope blurted, "being so tall."

"Hope Marie, that's enough of that sort of talk," Mrs. Mullen said. "It isn't polite to speak of a person's stature."

"Oh, I don't mean it as a bad thing, Mother," Hope said, and smiled at Heck admiringly. "Not at all. I love how tall you are, Heck. It's very impressive. And you look skinny, but your muscles are like iron."

"Hope," Mrs. Mullen said with a disapproving tone.

A blushing Hope kept smiling at Heck but said no more.

The Mullens had a nice little farm and a beautiful house that seemed like a mansion compared to Heck's old cabin and other places he'd stopped and stayed.

Mr. Mullen asked Heck about his life and teased out the details of how he had come to be riding alone.

The Mullens were clearly moved by his story.

Hope pointed to his shoulder. "Is that rip in your shirt from the bullet?"

Heck nodded. "Yes, ma'am."

Tom leaned closer. "Can I see it?"

"Sure," Heck said, spreading the torn fabric. "It's pretty well healed up now."

Tom whistled. "That must've hurt."

"At first, I was so mad, I couldn't even feel it," Heck said, then grinned. "Then, afterward, yeah, it started hurting like a horse bite."

Hope batted her long lashes at him. "You must be awful brave."

Heck smiled back at her, but his face burned with embarrassment, and he couldn't think of anything to say.

"That's the way it is in a fight," Mr. Mullen said, coming to life in a new way. He raised his fists and grinned. Like the rest of his family, he was small and red-haired. Despite his lack of size, there was no weakness in him, and Heck saw the man had big, scarred knuckles. "You don't really feel the pain until it's over. Or at least until between the rounds."

"Dad was a boxer," Tom said. "That's how he bought this land and built our house."

"The fight game was good to me," Mr. Mullen said, "but it's a hard life. If you'll do us the pleasure of staying with us for a few days, Heck, I'd be happy to show you the ropes, teach you a few combinations."

Heck glanced automatically to Mrs. Mullen, not wanting to impose.

She smiled and nodded.

"I would like that," Heck said.

"That's wonderful," Hope said. "I'll sew up your shirt for you, then."

For some reason, Mrs. Mullen grinned at her daughter. "That's very nice of you, Hope, but you can help me make Heck a new set of clothes instead. After all, he did get his old clothes muddy helping us. It's the least we can do."

"We have extra leather," Tom said. "Could I make Heck some boots?"

"That's a wonderful idea, Tom," Mrs. Mullen said.

"You helped the right family, Heck," Mr. Mullen said. "Young Tom here has a knack for leatherwork. Only sixteen, and he already earns a man's wage, cobbling shoes and making saddles and tack."

"Thank you all very much," Heck said. "I've never owned a real pair of boots before."

"I'll make you the best boots you'll ever wear," Tom said with obvious pride. "And if you like, I'll work on your saddle so it fits you just right."

"That sure would be nice. But I don't have the money for that."

"I wouldn't take pay if you did have money, Heck," Tom said. "It's my pleasure to help you like you helped us."

"So, Heck," Mr. Mullen said, as Heck dug into his second plate. "Where were you headed, anyway?"

Heck finished chewing then dabbed at the corners of his mouth with his napkin the way he'd seen the Mullens do. "West, sir."

"That narrows it down a touch," Mr. Mullen said. "What I mean to ask, however, is what point west of here were you fixed upon?"

"*The* West, sir."

"Ah, the West," Mr. Mullen said, and his eyes lit with fire as they had when he'd spoken of boxing. "Oregon Territory?"

Heck shrugged. "I don't know, sir. I've just heard the West is a good place to go."

"Aye, that it is, lad, that it is. A man can be his own boss in Oregon, that's for sure, and if I don't miss the mark of you, you're a lad who will be wanting to be his own boss."

"Yes, sir."

"Good, good," Mr. Mullen said. "Oregon's a paradise from what they say. Rich ground, practically free for the taking. Streams full of trout and salmon. Big timber, loads of game, deep soil as black as midnight. Men are making a fortune trapping, too, and setting things up for those who will follow. And mark my words, lad, folks will follow. They're going in droves now, big wagon trains, cutting across the prairie."

Mrs. Mullen looked serious. "Such a dangerous voyage."

"Aye, that it is," Mr. Mullen said, nodding, "what with the weather and bandits and Indians and all manner of deprivation. How would you go it alone, lad?"

Heck spread his big hands. "I hoped maybe I'd run into some other folks heading that way."

"We should go with Heck," Hope blurted.

Mr. Mullen nodded with a wistful smile. "I would love to, my darling. I surely would. And perhaps one day we will travel west, just as my own dear parents traveled west for a better life."

Mr. Mullen shook his head. As the man started speaking again, Heck realized Mr. Mullen had been dreaming of heading west for some time. "But it won't be this year, lass. It's too late.

We're plowing and planting and we've made no preparations. We'd have to sell the farm and buy a wagon and a whole mountain of provisions. I've heard tell it costs $500 to make the trip."

Heck choked a little when he heard the cost. Having been born way back in the holler, he'd never seen more than five dollars in his whole life.

Reading Heck's reaction, Mr. Mullen nodded with a knowing smile. "It's an expensive proposition, lad. If you want to see the West, head to St. Louis."

"I thought the wagon trains left out of Independence," Tom said.

"They do, son. But the trains have already left, and unless I am mistaken, our young friend is a few shillings shy of five hundred dollars."

Heck nodded, feeling foolish. How had he let himself believe he could head west?

And yet, even as he chastised himself, his heart remained set upon the goal.

"Head for St. Louis, lad. It's a mighty big town. You'll find work there. Work that'll pay cash. Work hard, save every penny you can, and in a few years, maybe you'll have enough to head west."

"Why does it cost so much?" Tom asked.

"There is much to buy," Mr. Mullen said. "A wagon, a team of oxen, and a whole mountain of provisions. And when you join a train, you have to pay the wagon master. He knows the way and understands the dangers, hires scouts, and gets you through to the promised land."

"Maybe you could hire on as a scout, Heck," Hope said with another admiring smile.

"Thanks for saying so, but I doubt it," Heck said. "I'm only fourteen."

"You're only fourteen?" Hope said, sounding both surprised and delighted. "That's how old I am. I thought you were seventeen or eighteen."

Heck shook his head. "I'll be fifteen in a couple of months."

"Fourteen," Mr. Mullen said, grinning at him. "My wife will surely disapprove of my addressing your stature, young man, but you certainly are big for your age. How tall are you?"

"I don't know, sir. Over six feet, I think."

"Oh yes, you're over six feet," Mr. Mullen said. "You go ahead and enjoy your dinner, and then, while Mrs. Mullen cuts the pie, we'll measure you."

After dinner, they gathered a chair and a pencil and the tape Tom used with his leather work. Mr. Mullen told Heck to stand with his back to the wall. Then he and his children set to measuring and marking.

"You're six feet, four inches tall, Heck!" Hope announced excitedly from atop the chair, her pretty face mere inches from his own.

"Lord have mercy," Mr. Mullen said, shaking his head. "Six foot four and only fourteen years old. You help me in the field these next few days, Heck, and I'll teach you to box. With a reach like yours, you'll make five hundred dollars in no time!"

CHAPTER 5

"That's it, lad," Mr. Mullen said, as Heck shuffled to his left, throwing another sequence of crisp jabs.

His target, a canvas bag Mr. Mullen had stuffed with sand and straw and sackcloth, hopped with every punch, and swayed back and forth, suspended from the beam by a thick rope.

"Power is good, but speed beats power, and timing beats speed," Mr. Mullen said from beside him. "Time the swing of the bag and wallop it with your right."

Heck nodded, cracked the bag with a stiff jab, and watched it swing away. When it swung back his way, he hammered it with a hard right.

"Oh, what a fighter you could be," Mr. Mullen said. "Six foot four, one hundred and fifty pounds, with the speed of a lightweight and the reach and power of a heavyweight."

Pleased, Heck had the sense to say nothing.

Mr. Mullen said, "Any man can make a fist, though, and learn to throw fast, hard punches. But that doesn't matter. What matters is how you handle yourself when someone is throwing punches back at you. Can you take a punch?"

Heck shrugged and pointed to the pale scar that split one dark eyebrow. "I got kicked by a mule once. It knocked me down, but I got back up."

Mr. Mullen laughed and slapped him on the back. "If you got up from a mule kick, lad, you could be a champion."

For the last week, Mr. Mullen had been teaching Heck the art of pugilism: how to stand, how to move, how to throw his punches in combinations, and how to spot and counter his opponent's various attacks. It was a lot to cover, but Heck took to it like a raccoon takes to sweet corn.

The first day, they'd spent a couple of hours with it after working in the field.

The second day, Mr. Mullen had insisted they knock off at noon, and they spent the rest of their time boxing.

The rest of the week, they'd barely finished family worship and started working before Mr. Mullen dragged him in the barn for more instruction.

Heck reckoned it was a good thing he was moving on, or the farm might go fallow.

But two nights earlier, Mrs. Mullen had suggested a departure date, framing it politely with "Tom should have your boots and saddle finished by then."

Mrs. Mullen didn't dislike Heck. He was sure of that. Quite the opposite, in fact. She treated him like her own son.

She wasn't blind, however. And if he were her own son, he would be welcome to stay forever, because she wouldn't be worried about something happening between Heck and Hope.

Although it still seemed impossible to him that such a

bright, beautiful, pure-hearted girl could have any interest in a raggedy mountain boy like himself, Hope was clearly sweet on him.

And every time Heck saw Hope, every time she spoke, every time he even heard someone else speak her name, his heart set to tumbling like a rock bouncing down a steep sidehill.

At mealtime, when Heck and the family sat down to eat together, none of this was lost on Mrs. Mullen. As Hope praised Heck and batted her lashes at him, her mother watched with knowing eyes.

The Mullens were a wonderful family, and Heck wouldn't do anything to disturb their peaceful, loving home, so when Mrs. Mullen made her not-so-subtle suggestion, he nodded and said he'd be leaving then and very happy to have the improved saddle and his first pair of boots for the trip.

Hope and Mrs. Mullen had already made him two new shirts, two pairs of trousers, and two sets of underwear.

"Ah, I'll be sorry to see you go, lad," Mr. Mullen said, handing him a wet towel for his scuffed and bleeding knuckles. "Tell me, will you be taking my advice and heading to St. Louis?"

"Yes, sir."

"Aye, that's a good lad. It's the best thing for you, mark my words. Head to St. Louis and build up a stake before heading west."

"I'll do it, sir."

"Good. But listen, Heck. When you get to St. Louis, look up a man by the name of Paddy Corcoran. Tell him you're a proud son of Ireland, fighting out of the mountains and sent by none other than Tommy Mullen, d'you understand?"

Heck nodded. "Yes, sir."

"That's a lad. Prizefighting is a tough way to make a living. Trust me. Look at my ears. Look at my nose. Look at all the scar tissue over my eyes. It's a tough life, and you need someone you can trust to help you through. Most managers are snakes. They handle fighters like a butcher handles a side of beef. But you can trust good old Paddy."

Heck wasn't sure he would actually try boxing. It seemed like a hard and dangerous way to make money. But he appreciated Mr. Mullen's efforts, and after days of home-cooked meals, he felt strong enough to punch holes in granite. One way or the other, he promised to send the Mullens letters from St. Louis to let them know how he was doing.

He would miss them. He would miss working and training alongside Mr. Mullen and hearing his lilting voice, which always glowed with good humor. He would miss playing chess with Tom during evenings and would miss the motherly warmth of Mrs. Mullen. Most of all, however, he would miss Hope, whose slightest smile warmed his soul and whose every move, no matter how subtle, commanded his eyes and his imagination.

But it was time to go.

That night, they had a wonderful supper together, and Hope joined Tom and Heck while they played chess then strolled outside to sit with Heck and Mrs. Mullen, who was knitting on the porch.

Heck and Hope talked idly, never seeming to have anything to talk about but never running out of things to say. She did most of the talking, and he loved to sit back and listen to her stories and just to hear her voice, which was to him the sound of angels singing.

That night, lying in bed thinking about Hope, he heard a noise in the hall beyond his door. A floorboard creaked then fell silent.

He lay there, straining his ears, wondering if he'd actually heard anything, his heart beating quickly for some strange reason.

For a while, there was only silence.

Then another floorboard creaked, and his door rattled gently against its jam.

Was someone standing just outside his door?

Heck rose silently from the bed, crossed the darkened room, and laid his ear against the door, listening hard.

He stood there for several seconds, heart thumping hard, and heard only the sound of his own breathing. Then he became aware of another sound—another person's breathing just on the other side of the door—and he knew that person was pressed into the door just as he was, their trembling bodies separated by only an inch of wood.

"Heck?"

Hope's whisper startled and thrilled him.

"Heck, are you there?"

"Yeah," he said, and his own whisper sounded strange to his ears, as if he had something stuck in his throat. "I'm here, Hope."

"I wish you weren't leaving."

"I know. I wish I could stay."

She was silent for a second.

Heck wanted to open the door and… what? Take her in his

arms? Kiss her? He didn't know. Those ideas sounded mighty nice, but he would never disrespect Hope or her family.

"Are you still there?" Hope whispered.

"Yeah, I'm still here."

"I'm gonna miss you, Heck. I think I…" She trailed off into silence.

He waited.

After several seconds of silence, he began to fear she'd left.

Then she whispered his name again.

"Yeah?"

"Are you gonna miss me, Heck?"

"You know I am."

"Say it."

"I'm gonna miss you, Hope. I'm gonna miss you real bad."

"Thank you for saying it, Heck."

"I mean it."

"I know you do. I mean it, too. But I reckon I'd best get back to bed. Mama will have a cow if she catches me out here. Goodnight, Heck."

"Goodnight, Hope."

CHAPTER 6

The next day, the Mullens sent Heck off in grand fashion. Mrs. Mullen made a big breakfast of eggs and sausage and fried potatoes with buttered toast and strawberry preserves.

Everyone was excited for him. Everyone except Hope, that is. She barely spoke a word and every time she looked at him, tears glistened in her emerald eyes.

Abruptly, Hope stood. "Please excuse me, everyone. I'm going to saddle Dolly and take a ride."

Mrs. Mullen frowned at her daughter. "Don't you want to say goodbye to Heck?"

"No," Hope said, shaking her head. "I don't ever want to say goodbye. I hate that he's leaving." She turned to Heck with tears streaming down her cheeks and took a deep breath, gathering herself. "I'm sorry, Heck. Goodbye. I'm going to miss you."

"I'm gonna miss you, too, Hope," Heck said, but the door was already swinging shut after Hope, who had rushed outside.

"Please excuse Hope," Mrs. Mullen said. "She's just sad to see you go."

After lunch, they went out to the barn stall Tom had converted into a leatherworking area. The smell there was wonderful, a combination of old hay and new leather.

Tom smiled proudly and handed Heck a beautiful pair of boots.

For a moment, Heck could only stare in wonder.

Laughing, Mr. Mullen slapped Heck on the back. "I told you he has the knack."

Heck nodded, grinning like a fool. "Thank you, Tom. I never expected anything like this. I don't know what to say."

"You already said thanks," Tom said. "That's plenty. Besides, your smile says it all. I'm glad you like them, Heck. I hope they'll protect your feet during your Western adventures. Try them on."

Heck sat down on a stool and pulled on the right boot. He'd never felt anything like it. His heart soared. He had real boots!

"I made them a touch big," Tom admitted, "so you'll have room to grow, since you're only fourteen."

"That was smart," Heck said. "Thank you."

"And since I knew Tom was making them a bit large, I knitted these for you," Mrs. Mullen said, handing Heck two pairs of heavy wool socks.

"Thank you so much, ma'am. You have all been so kind to me."

"We never would have had the chance if you had passed us by when we were in need," Mrs. Mullen said. "Good folks help one another. That's the way of the world. Now, let me go back to the kitchen and finish packing some food for you to take on your trip."

Heck thanked her then shook Tom's hand and set to saddling Annabelle.

Mr. Mullen walked out with him.

At the gate, Mr. Mullen handed Heck a fat leather pouch that clinked with coins. "There's five dollars inside."

Heck gawked at it. "Mr. Mullen, that's a lot of money. I can't take it."

"Sure you can, lad. Take it. You've earned it. It's your wages for a week's work."

"But you put me up and fed me and taught me to box."

"And I loved every second. Now take the money. It's bad luck to refuse a gift."

Heck pocketed the pouch. "Thank you, Mr. Mullen, for everything."

"It was our pleasure. Now, don't forget to write. Unlike you, I never learned to read, but the rest of the family can read your letters to me. You have the address, don't you?"

"Yes, sir." He patted his shirt pocket, where he'd tucked the Mullens' address, then stuck out his hand. "Thanks again."

Mr. Mullen seized his hand, gave it a good squeeze, then hauled Heck into an embrace. "You're a good lad, Heck, and I'm excited to hear what you make of your life. Whatever it is, you're destined for greatness, son. On that, I'd bet my last penny."

Heck rode off, feeling a rush of powerful emotions.

Foremost among these was gratitude. The Mullens had treated him like a member of their own family.

When he'd waded into that creek, he'd had next to nothing.

Now, he had clothes, boots, five dollars in his pocket, a basic understanding of boxing, a contact in St. Louis, and a plan.

He would go find this Paddy Corcoran, learn to box, and hopefully earn enough money to set out on the Oregon Trail in a few years.

Optimism filled him. Partly because he had a plan, partly because he was an optimist by nature, and partly because of the slip of paper in his shirt pocket.

By giving him that address and making him promise to write, Mr. Mullen had given Heck a powerful reason to succeed. Heck already hungered for a good life; but now, having agreed to write the Mullens, he was determined to fill those letters with good news.

He imagined Hope reading his letters aloud to a smiling Mr. Mullen, imagined all the Mullens nodding and saying they knew Heck was special. That was a vision worth fighting for.

They say when a boy doesn't have a father, he must make one for himself; and that's what Heck did then, framing his future and his expectations of himself in terms of the news he could send back to the Mullens.

Sometimes, that's all it takes for a boy to become a man: the knowledge that someone will be waiting to hear from him and hoping for good news.

Amidst these waves of gratitude and this flood of optimistic determination, a powerful sense of loss pierced his heart. How he would miss the Mullens… especially Hope.

He hated the way they parted and could still remember her reddish-brown locks fluttering as she'd fled the house.

Memory stirred in Heck, and he traveled back to the previous night, when he stood against the door, breathing in unison with Hope, their bodies almost touching. He remembered their whispered conversation and wished he'd opened the door if only to have one more memory of her beautiful face.

He pictured Hope's face now, his heart throbbing with loss. He could all but see the long lashes and moss-green eyes flecked with amber; the delicate spray of light freckles that danced across the bridge of her nose and high cheekbones; her small mouth with its full, soft-looking lips that spread so easily for him, revealing the bright and shining treasure of her smile.

It was a face he could study every day for the rest of his life and still find himself wanting more.

This powerful sense of loss also opened floodgates for pent-up pain out of the past. He had never really grieved his father, never really allowed himself to examine that terrible loss.

The loss of Hope and her family primed the pump, and the loss of his father and mother exploded from his heart in a geyser of grief that half choked him and made his vision go blurry with involuntary tears. When he couldn't blink these away, he dried his eyes with the sleeve of his new shirt.

Heck took a deep breath and let it shudder free and forced his mind to focus on all the many good things in his life and the future awaiting him, and as he rode down the sun-dappled lane with its latticework of light and shade falling through the limbs overhead, his spirits lifted as if they were joining the cheerful sound of birdsong that stitched the air in all directions.

A moment later, he heard hooves pounding on the trail behind him, coming up fast, and he twisted in his saddle and lowered one hand to the flintlock pistol he'd freshly charged for his trip, ready for anything.

CHAPTER 7

When the hard-charging rider rounded the corner behind Heck, he saw not the snarling face of a highwayman but the angelic face he had just been conjuring and savoring in his mind.

"Hope," he said, as she drew her horse up next to his.

Hope's auburn locks were in a state of lovely disarray. Her green eyes, swollen with tears, locked onto him, shining more brightly than ever from a face pink with emotion. Hope lifted her chin, and her gaze hardened with determination as she sidled her horse against Annabelle and stared directly into his eyes.

A warm spring breeze ruffled their clothing, and Hope pinned her hat to her head.

"Heck Martin," she said, "I want you to kiss me."

Just like that, Heck's face was hot as a skillet. "I can't do that, Hope. Your daddy would skin me alive."

"Daddy won't know. Just a quick kiss, Heck? Please? I've

never kissed a boy before, and you're the only boy in the whole world I ever want to kiss."

Heck chuckled self-consciously, feeling nervous and excited and vaguely confused. "I never kissed a girl, either."

For some reason, this made Hope smile. "You haven't? I figured you'd probably done a lot of kissing."

Heck shook his head. "Not ever. I lived way back in the holler. I barely even saw girls."

Hope's smile widened, and that playful look came into her eyes, softening them in a wonderful way. "Well, I hereby stake my claim, Mr. Martin."

She reached up and latched onto the back of his neck and pulled his face down to hers and planted a kiss right on his lips.

Heck went rigid, his whole body filled instantly with warmth and light and happiness, as if her kiss had lit a furnace of joy he hadn't even known resided within him.

Hope studied his frozen face with a look of concern. "What's the matter, Heck? Didn't I do it right? Didn't you like it?"

"Oh, I liked it," he said, finally coming to life. "I liked it a lot. I was just surprised was all. Come on back over here and let's try that again."

He lowered his face to hers. Their mouths met, and their lips moved together, lingering in a slow, sweet kiss that cranked the light and heat and happiness of the furnace within Heck.

After a long and joyous time, Hope leaned back and stared up, smiling ecstatically and leaking tears at the same time.

Heck wondered why she would smile and cry at the same time but reminded himself that he knew nothing about girls. Maybe they had an extra emotion that men lacked, something that combined happiness and sorrow.

Whatever the case, he reached out, took her lovely face in his hands, and gently wiped away her tears.

"I want to see you again, Heck," she said.

"We'll see each other again."

"You promise?"

"I promise."

"I want to marry you."

Heck laughed. "Marry me?"

Hope's eyes flashed. "You don't have to laugh at me for loving you."

"Love? We just met." But even as he spoke these words, Heck knew what Hope meant. He felt something, too, that furnace in his chest and below it, something like a ball of hot wax melting in his stomach. Was that love?

"You don't love me?" she asked.

"I didn't say that."

"You said we just met."

"Well, we did just meet."

"Yeah, but you know what I mean."

"You just surprised me was all."

She tilted her face, half-grinning. "You sure do surprise easy."

"I guess you just have a gift for surprising me."

"Well, I hope that never changes."

"I can't imagine it will. Something tells me you will always be full of surprises."

"You want to kiss me again?"

"Worse than I want to breathe."

He started to lean forward, but Hope leaned back.

"You really don't love me, Heck?"

He thought about that for a moment, examining not only her beautiful face and his urge to kiss her but also the red-hot furnace and that hot wax feeling inside himself and the way he'd been mourning her after they had parted, as if he'd left a part of himself back on the Mullen farm.

A big smile stretched across his face. "You know what? Now that I think about it, I do love you. I really do."

Hope gave a happy squeal and leaned in not to kiss him but to wrap him up in a big hug.

He hugged her back, loving the feel of her in his arms.

"I love you, too, Heck. I love you with all my heart, and you're the only man I will ever love. Will you really write?"

"You know I will."

"My parents won't let me marry yet."

There she was, talking about marriage again. The notion jarred him, but once he let it settle, it didn't bother him a bit. "All right."

"All right?" She leaned back again, frowning. "Don't you want to marry me?"

"You sure have a way of twisting my words around. I'd love to marry you, Hope."

She smiled. "I'd love to marry you, too, Heck, and that's just what I'm going to do."

"How? I'm gonna be up in St. Louis, and then I'm heading out West."

"I don't know how yet, but you mark my words, we are going to be married. As Daddy always says, where there's a will, there's a way, and I have all the will in the world when it comes to marrying you."

At that moment, they heard another rider approaching and without a word separated their horses by a few feet.

"That'll be Tom," Hope said, "or maybe Daddy. Say it one more time before he gets here, Heck?"

"Say what?"

"You know what, silly."

"I love you, Hope."

Her face lit up brighter and more beautiful than ever. "I love you, too, Heck, and someday, you're going to be my husband."

CHAPTER 8

Heck and Annabelle crossed the Mississippi by ferry, and suddenly, they were in the West.

A short time later, Heck encountered his first trouble since leaving Detwiler behind.

Heck didn't like something about the men as soon as he came over the rise and saw them standing in the road fifty or sixty yards farther on.

They looked raggedy and sullen, one big, one small. The big one held a rifle or a shotgun. Heck couldn't tell at that distance.

But his gut told him something was wrong. Maybe it was how the men looked, standing there, blocking his way. Maybe it was because neither of them hailed him the way all those friendly Kentuckians had. Or maybe the good Lord just blessed Heck with an instinct for danger.

Whatever the case, Heck didn't trust them, and moving slowly so as not to reveal his actions, he pulled the flintlock from his belt, laid it across the saddle horn, and drew back the hammer, careful to keep his finger away from the trigger.

As Heck drew closer, he saw the smaller man was actually a boy around his age. The boy held a hatchet much like the one in Heck's haversack.

Yeah, these two were up to no good.

Heck considered trying to race past them, but the road was none too wide, and they looked like hard folks. If he tried, he figured the man would blow him out of the saddle.

Heck reined up fifteen feet from where they stood.

"Afternoon," the man said without smiling.

Heck nodded but said nothing, that icy calm settling over him again. Once more, the world around him seemed to move at half pace, while Heck's mind and body stood apart, reading everything, ready to react.

He noticed the boy's nervous grin, the way he kept shifting his weight from foot to foot, and the white-knuckled grip he had on the hatchet.

Heck also noticed the man's hard eyes flicking back and forth, studying him, probably looking for weapons, before flicking up the road, studying Heck's back trail, wanting to make sure that no one was following. As the man checked these things, his barrel drifted slowly, almost imperceptibly, up.

"You traveling alone?" he asked.

"No, sir. Me and my brothers and our pa. They'll be along directly."

The man grinned at that. "You lie."

Now, in Kentucky of 1847, the man had just given Heck the right to shoot him dead. But of course, this was Missouri, Heck had lied, and he was new to violence such as this, so he just sat there holding the old pistol out of view and said nothing.

"This here's a toll road," the man said.

The kid nodded, his grin still nervous but growing meaner by the second.

Heck wasn't nervous at all, only sharp and ready.

"How much?" Heck asked, figuring it'd be worth a penny to be rid of this pair.

"How much you got?" the man asked with a grin missing most of its teeth, and Heck knew how this was going to go.

The man shouldered the rifle and started to bring the barrel around, so Heck lifted the flintlock and pulled the trigger.

Annabelle reared up and threw Heck. He hit the ground hard. It knocked the wind out of him, but he knew he couldn't lay there feeling sorry for himself.

He sat up, holding the flintlock in both hands, then realized his shot and powder were in his haversack, which had ridden off atop Annabelle.

The man was down, one arm poking up kind of crooked like a pitchfork left in fresh-tilled soil. The rifle lay beside him. One foot was twitching back and forth, but that was it.

The boy was nowhere in sight. Heck heard him crashing away into a roadside thicket.

Heck stood, managed to draw a breath, and approached the man, who had quit twitching.

Annabelle was way down the road, stepping high and shaking her head and snorting.

Heck was about to call to her when snapping branches and waggling weeds told him the kid was coming back. He burst onto the road twenty feet away with the hatchet in his hand and a look of wild desperation in his eyes.

Heck picked up the dead man's rifle, pointed it at him, and said in a calm voice, "You get on out of here, or I'll kill you, too."

He must've taken Heck at his word, because he plunged back into the brush quick as a jackrabbit.

Looking down at the dead man, Heck felt no remorse. The highwayman would have killed him if Heck hadn't fired first.

So no, Heck didn't feel remorse. But he did feel a sense of urgency. These two might have kin close by, after all.

Heck searched the bandit's pockets but found only a rusty clasp knife, the shot pouch and powder horn for the single-shot squirrel gun, and a brick of cornbread wrapped up in a handkerchief.

Heck took it all, slung the rifle over his shoulder, and talked real soft to Annabelle until she came back to him. Then he rode off, hoping to put some distance between him and these folks before dark.

A few miles down the road, Heck realized he did have to say one thing for that highwayman. The cornbread ended up being pretty good.

CHAPTER 9

Almost a year later...

The stout man in the red sweater hollered, "Weighing in at one hundred and sixty pounds, with an impressive record of nineteen wins, zero losses, all nineteen victories coming by way of knockout, Heck 'Mountain Man' Martin!"

The men gathered behind the smoky riverfront warehouse cheered raucously, laughing and sloshing beer, ready for blood.

The stout man announced, "His opponent, tipping the scales at a powerful one hundred and ninety pounds, the fighting pride of New Orleans and heavyweight champion of the West, with a remarkable record of fifty-seven wins against only three defeats, 'Hammering' Hank Mitchell."

The crowd roared with approval as Heck's burly opponent lifted his big fists overhead.

Heck examined the man across the ring, studying him for any weaknesses. This he had learned to do over the violent year he'd spent in St. Louis.

Following Mr. Mullen's advice, he had tracked down the experienced boxing trainer, Paddy Corcoran, who had taken Heck under his wing as soon as he'd heard Mr. Mullen's name.

Heck was a quick student, and Corcoran taught him to fight like a champion. They used gloves for sparring, saving Heck from cutting his face and breaking his knuckles, and a short time later, he was boxing grown men in St. Louis saloons and aboard Mississippi riverboats.

At first, the fights were based on spectacle. There was no shortage of men ready to step into the ring against a tall, skinny boy of only fourteen years.

Most of his fights were against local loudmouths, big men who hit hard but didn't know much about fighting. Heck beat them quickly and easily, surprising everyone with his speed, power, and skill.

Because he won so easily, Heck fought every week or two in those early days and made a surprising amount of money between prizes and betting.

After winning fifteen fights, however, Heck was no longer a waterfront oddity. Word spread that the toughest man in Missouri was actually not a man at all but merely a tall boy with quick hands.

His last four fights were against actual boxers, men who knew how to fight and made Heck work for his money. These fighters knew not only how to punch but how to feint; could not only take hard shots but evade them as well; and when he rocked them, they were wise enough to cast pride aside and take a knee, ending the round and gaining thirty seconds of rest.

Even though Heck bested them all, these fights were longer

and harder. His fight against Jack Baxter, a 180-pounder from Ohio, was a brutal, 38-round affair that ended with a bloodied Baxter unconscious for several minutes.

It had taken Heck three months to fully recover from that fight.

He'd spent much of that time wandering St. Louis aimlessly, dreaming of the West and rereading the few letters he'd received from the Mullens.

Mrs. Mullen wrote the letters, but Tom and Hope included short notes in the postscript.

Hope could not confess her feelings, of course, but she always wished him well and included things that made him feel like she still loved him and wanted to marry him.

"Nothing has changed for me," she would write. "I think of you constantly, miss you terribly, and cannot wait to see you again in the future."

All winter, he hoped he would receive a letter saying the family would be heading west this spring. But he had received no such letter. The Mullens would remain on their farm in Kentucky.

Heck, on the other hand, would head west—if he won this fight.

The excitement of the Bloody Island crowd confirmed what Heck had already guessed. The spectators would bet heavily on Mitchell. And why wouldn't they? He was much bigger than Heck and had three times as many fights.

Yes, they would bet heavily on the heavyweight champ, giving anyone foolish enough to bet on Heck 10-1 odds.

Which is why Heck—who had traveled to New Orleans,

watched Mitchell fight, and devised a plan—had bet the entirety of his $1300 savings on himself.

He already had plenty of money to head west, but he wanted enough money to not only travel in style but also purchase large tracts of land and anything he and the Mullens might need if they ever joined him on the new frontier.

Though Heck was only fifteen, he had no fear. God had given him certain gifts, including a granite chin, long arms, and extreme height.

Seeing his long, lean frame, everyone expected Heck to dance behind a jab, but God had also given him tremendous power in both hands.

Mitchell marched around the ring, strutting like a fighting rooster. He was six inches shorter than Heck with wide shoulders and a thick chest matted in what looked like fur.

As Mitchell paraded around the ring, the now familiar icy calm settled over Heck, slowing the world and giving him the chance to study his opponent, judging his reach, noting the heavy scar tissue over the right eye, and reading the punching power suggested by Mitchell's muscular thighs.

"For the love of all that's holy," Corcoran said, as Heck pulled the leather string from his neck and handed over his mother's golden ring for safekeeping during the fight, "use your reach tonight. Keep him off with the jab, and it'll be an easy fight. But if you let him inside..."

"It'll be okay," Heck said.

"Don't be so sure. He's the best you've faced. You have to be careful."

Heck chuckled. Corcoran was a good manager, but he

always got nervous before a fight. And, as always, Heck's unflappable calm only made Corcoran more anxious.

"Have to watch out," Corcoran said as the referee called the fighters to the center of the ring. "Especially in the early rounds. He's a crafty veteran with a reputation as a dirty brawler. He—"

"Gentlemen," the ref said as Heck and Mitchell reached the center of the ring.

Mitchell grinned cockily up at Heck, his smile full of gaps where his teeth had been knocked out.

Heck looked back with no expression. He never played the games other fighters did, boasting and threatening and sneering before a fight. Heck preferred to let his fists do the talking.

"I want a clean fight," the ref said. "No headbutts, no elbows, no hitting below the belt. No kicking, no rabbit punches, no blows to the kidney. And Mitchell, no biting."

Mitchell laughed at that and bared his remaining teeth again.

"Are you hearing me, men?"

"He's no man," Mitchell snorted. "He's just a kid, and I'm gonna make him go nighty night."

They went to their respective corners, and everyone but the ref and fighters left the ring.

"Stick and move," Corcoran begged.

Billy, one of Heck's sparring partners and Corcoran's assistant tonight, slapped Heck on the back. "You know what to do, Heck."

Heck nodded at him, and the bell rang.

CHAPTER 10

The crowd hooted with excitement as Mitchell came racing across the ring, launching a barrage of wild haymakers.

Heck danced out of the way, pumping his jab defensively.

"That's it, Heck!" Corcoran shouted. "Just like that!"

For the next few minutes, Heck moved laterally and used his long jab to keep the wildly swinging Mitchell at bay.

The crowd booed, telling him to stand and fight.

If they want blood, Heck thought, clipping Mitchell with a jab and slipping outside another haymaker, *let them come in here and fight.*

He wasn't here to play puppet to the crowd; he was here to win and secure a future for himself and hopefully the Mullens.

Going toe to toe with a full-strength Mitchell would be foolish.

So Heck continued to circle the 24-foot ring and made the larger, older man chase him. Heck didn't throw a single hook or right hand, let alone an uppercut. He just kept pumping the lead hand.

The crowd screamed for action.

Heck blocked them out and concentrated on controlling his breathing as he dodged Mitchell's attacks.

Since no one had fallen, the round stretched on and on. Heck was pleased to see his aggressive opponent breathing hard and pleased again to see frustration growing on the man's red face.

Mitchell charged again.

Heck slipped a left and stepped straight into a looping right. The punch slammed into his jaw and drove him back into the ropes.

Mitchell had set him up. Now, the champion from New Orleans swarmed Heck, grabbed him around the midsection, and threw him to the ground, ending the first round.

The fighters went to their corners for a thirty-second break and a drink of water.

"Keep moving, kid," Corcoran said. "He's getting tired already."

"Time!" the ref called, and both men returned to the scratch mark at the center of the ring.

When the action started again, Heck leaned away from a shot that might have torn his chin off, and pivoted out of danger, jabbing as Mitchell whirled.

Heck's knuckles bounced off the heavyweight's scarred brow, but Mitchell stepped out at a sharp angle, cutting off Heck's retreat, and drove him into the ropes, hammering at his long body.

Heck covered his ribs and leaned away, expecting either a

body attack or an overhand shot, but Mitchell reared back his leering face and butted Heck hard in the solar plexus.

Pain filled Heck's chest, and much of the air rushed from his lungs.

"No butting, Mitchell!" the ref warned, separating the fighters.

"Shoulda stayed home tonight, boy," Mitchell growled, coming for Heck again.

Heck moved, snapping jabs, targeting the mass of scar tissue over his opponent's right eye. When fighting, there's always a temptation to get reckless after your opponent lands a good punch, and that goes double when you're fouled.

But despite his youth, Heck was too smart to give into emotion. He stuck to the plan, moving and jabbing, letting the crowd bellow as he kept Mitchell at bay.

The round stretched on and on. Five minutes, ten, more...

Breathing hard, Mitchell landed a few shots, mostly to the body, but nothing of consequence.

Heck kept moving and kept targeting the right eye, which was swelling now.

Mitchell's relentless pressure had won over the St. Louis crowd. They shouted at Heck, calling him a coward, not one of them tough enough to survive a single round against either of the men in the ring. But rules and ropes afford spectators great courage, so they continued to insult the young man battling a champion with a thirty-pound weight advantage.

Heck ignored them, moving smoothly behind a crisp jab until he finally saw what he'd been waiting for.

Mitchell was pawing at his swollen eye and struggling to get a deep breath. The champion had worn himself out pressing the fight. Swinging hard and hitting only air is utterly exhausting.

Meanwhile, Heck felt completely fresh. The predator in him came to life, savoring the signs of Mitchell's weakness.

Mitchell came plodding forward, still huffing and puffing, and a determined look on his face.

Heck flicked a jab, leaned away as if he was about to run again, then surprised everyone by standing his ground and cranking a hard left hook that nailed Mitchell in his swollen eye. A bad cut opened instantly, and Mitchell reeled backward.

Grinning fiercely, Heck pounced. He did not use his height or reach. He pressed forward, firing a combination of short hard punches, driving Mitchell into the ropes. Heck's fists pounded into his overwhelmed opponent's head from all angles.

Wild with desperation, Mitchell kneed Heck in the thigh, grappled him around the middle, and sunk his teeth into Heck's side.

Hollering, Heck shook free of the vicious attack then delivered a blistering uppercut that snapped Mitchell's head back.

It was the moment Heck had been waiting for, that sweet moment when you really hurt your opponent for the first time. He felt the punch thud home and felt the shock waves spread through Mitchell, felt the champion's body wobble and weaken.

Heck took half a step back, buying himself space to work, and threw a series of quick lefts and rights, favoring speed over power and targeting the head of Mitchell, who raised his guard high... just as Heck had known he would.

Then Heck launched his real attack, the attack he'd been setting up, and hammered the dirty fighter's midsection with several blistering hooks. The punches landed clean, and Heck felt the burly man's ribs snap beneath his knuckles.

Mitchell grunted and dropped his guard, hugging his broken ribs.

Heck caught him with a slashing right that spun his jaw straight into Heck's blistering left hook, which dropped the heavyweight to the ground and ended the round.

The traitorous crowd roared with glee and cheered for Heck.

Heck went to his corner and watched his opponent's cornermen try to lift Mitchell to his feet. Failing that, they dragged the unconscious man to his corner and did their best to rouse him from his stupor.

After thirty seconds, the referee called, "Time," which meant the fighters had eight seconds to return to the scratch.

Heck went to the mark and waited.

Mitchell was awake, but while his cornermen shouted at him, the heavyweight merely shook his head and clutched his shattered ribs.

The referee finished his count and raised Heck's hand in the air, announcing there was a new heavyweight champion of the West.

Heck didn't care about the championship. He did care about the West, though, and suddenly, he had enough money to buy a good chunk of it.

CHAPTER 11

Heck rode out of St. Louis on a big, red stallion with a scattergun in one scabbard and a brand new, St. Louis-made, .54 caliber Hawken rifle in the other. A six-shot .44 Walker Colt rode on his hip. On his opposite hip, he wore a big fighting knife in a heavy leather sheathe.

Trailing behind him, the pack mule was loaded with everything he figured he'd need for the ride to Independence, where he would purchase the rest of his equipment and finally start his journey to the far West.

He knew he would arrive a little late in the season but still hoped to join forces with a wagon train.

After a year of fighting and betting on his own matches, he had over $13,000, an unthinkable sum with which he could easily buy a massive farm, build a house, purchase tools and livestock, and hire more help than he would ever need; but that life held no appeal to him now. No other life could hold any appeal until he had tried his luck in the West.

Morning, noon, and night, that's what he had dreamed of and fought for. That and someday reuniting with the Mullens, though the latter dream had faded a bit, seeing as the family had not chosen to head west this spring.

That meant the Mullens wouldn't be making the trip for at least another year. By then, Hope would be sixteen and mobbed with suitors, and Heck supposed she would forget all about him.

So he fixed his mind on the West and rode off with only the vaguest notion of what he would do when he reached the promised land.

He had no concern about starving. Everyone reported plentiful game along the way, and Heck had been hunting since he was old enough to shoulder a musket.

He'd already put a few dozen rounds through the Hawken, and it was a thing of beauty. The first afternoon, he'd gotten used to the weight, the kick, and the double trigger. The first pull set the hammer, creating a hair trigger that increased accuracy.

With Pa's old Kentucky rifle, Heck had been able to part a gnat's hair at 100 yards. With the Hawken, he could trim that same gnat's sideburns at 400.

From St. Louis, he followed the Missouri River and two weeks later arrived at Independence to beautiful weather and bitter disappointment.

Most of the wagon trains had left weeks earlier. Independence Square was churned up and loud with latecomers, who shouted and cursed, snapping whips too frequently, Heck thought, watching as teams of oxen plodded off, pulling awkwardly packed wagons owned by disorganized groups. The men looked flustered but determined. The women looked grim. Pale-faced children peered like tiny ghosts from the gloom of the wagons.

"Ain't none of my business," said the man Heck had been talking to, "but they gonna die, most of 'em." He leaned and spat a long, brown stream of tobacco juice into a wagon rut as if to emphasize his point.

"They don't look ready," Heck said.

"Nope. They ain't. Folks who was ready left weeks ago. These folks is just pretending is all. They got it in their mind to head west. Now, they paid their money, and nothing's gonna stop 'em till they're dead on the trail."

Heck nodded, wondering about his own shoddy preparation. He had good gear but no plan past this point. And seeing these folks ride off, he was no longer so keen on falling in with them.

The man glanced at Heck and his outfit. "You planning to throw in with these'uns?"

"I was," Heck confessed.

The man shook his head and spat again. "Not to tell you your business, young man, but unless you aim to drown or get scalped, steer clear of 'em. You hear how dangerous the trail is, how many folks die along the way, but I'll tell you the truth. Mostly, it's long and wearisome. The good wagon masters get through. But the good'uns already left. These folks here, they's the ones giving the trail a bad name. Look at 'em. They's determined to die."

Heck nodded, feeling truth come off the man's criticism. But he couldn't turn back now. He had come too far and invested too much of his heart and mind to retreat.

"I see the look in your eye, young man. Again, it's none of my business, but if you want to know what I think..."

"I do."

"Well, if you're bound and determined to head west, take that big red horse of yours and ride out in front of these folks. Between Westport and Council Grove, you'll come to Eleazer Plank's trading post on the river."

"All right."

"Old Eleazer does good business with the wagon trains, but he also trades a lot with mountain men who don't want to come this far east. Those men have their own ways. Like to be one or two still hanging around, waiting to head back out the trail. You throw in with one of them, maybe pay him a little, he'll get you where you want to go, catch you up with a train that knows what it's doin'."

"Thank you, sir. That sounds like a good plan."

After restocking supplies, Heck headed west. Because he was fifteen and an optimist by nature, he quickly latched onto this new plan.

He had a great horse and a Missouri mule. He had taken to calling them Red and Burly. All he needed now was an experienced guide to get him on down the trail, where he could join up with an experienced train.

He was surprised, as soon as he left Independence, by the amount of refuse littering the trail.

As he passed the less-experienced trains, folks waved and greeted him loudly. Heck lifted his hat but kept riding.

Over the next week, he made good time through country that was to him both beautiful and strange. Its beauty was indisputable, but to a boy who'd grown up in the mountains of

Kentucky, there was something forbidding in the flat openness of the grassland.

A few times along the trail, he camped with trains who'd already set up in the best spots. It was good to talk with folks and hear what they had to say, but it didn't take long during any of these stops to convince Heck he had made the right choice, striking out on his own.

He hoped the man back in Independence Square had exaggerated the likelihood of these kind folks dying, but he wouldn't bet his mule on it. For all their hope and hospitality, these folks pitched a rough camp, made a lot of noise, and seemed to have a hard time controlling their children and animals.

Each time he left their company, he felt like a heavy yoke had been lifted from his shoulders. At first, he had assumed this was simply the good feeling of being free again. Heck was nothing if not independent, after all.

But after leaving a very pleasant and very obviously ill-prepared train hailing from his home state, he realized the heavy yoke had little to do with regaining independence and much to do with departing before these folks started to die.

After that, Heck avoided the trains and camped alone.

CHAPTER 12

A cluster of low buildings the color of mud squatted alongside the river. Three mules with muddy shanks were tied beside a beautiful steeldust.

Heck approached the main building. Beneath a weather-beaten sign reading *PLANK'S POST,* seated upon the sagging porch that ran the length of the building, was the filthiest man Heck had ever seen.

Mud caked his boots, and curious stains mottled his buckskins, making them look like the hide of a discolored paint pony. The man eased back and forth in an old rocker, his hands and face dark with sun and grime, his wild, gray beard streaked in dark stains of indeterminate origin.

As Heck came up the steps, the smell of the man assaulted his nostrils. He managed not to wince, nodding politely instead. "Morning, sir. Would you be Mr. Plank?"

The gray beard broke apart as the man cackled wildly and slapped the thighs of his greasy buckskins. "Sonny, if'n I were

Eleazer Plank, I sure wouldn't be wasting my twilight years sitting on this old porch. I'd be set up pretty as you please with half a dozen squaws and a larder full of cakes and pickles. Old Eleazer's richer than King Nebuchadnezzar!"

As the filthy man fell into another cackling fit, Heck nodded and went inside, relieved to escape the laughter and stench.

Heck spotted a counter at the opposite end of the large room. Behind it, a gray-haired man spoke with a young woman who sat on a stool nearby, seeming to ignore him. Heck couldn't hear the man's words, but irritation was plain in the man's voice.

Heck headed in that direction. Passing three rough-looking men standing by the flour, he nodded.

The men just stared back, their eyes hard and calculating.

Having spent the last year in the crime-ridden city of St. Louis, Heck instantly understood this trio would feel no qualms about hurting folks and taking what they wanted.

He figured he'd best take care of business quickly and get on his way. If they left before him, he'd have to head outside and make sure the trio didn't steal Red and Burly and everything attached to them—including the $13,000 he had stashed away beneath false bottoms in his saddle bags and the pocket he'd had sewn into the back of his saddle.

He carried the rest on his person, $100 in a money belt and $30 more in his pockets.

"Morning," the gray-haired man said as Heck approached. The young woman rose with no expression on her face and disappeared into a door behind the man. "I'm Eleazer Plank. What can I do for you?"

"Morning, Mr. Plank. My name's Heck Martin. I need to pick up a few supplies."

"Well, you come to the right place, young man. What d'ya need?"

"A little of this, a little of that," Heck said, aware that the three men behind him had edged closer to watch and listen.

With a casual movement of his hand, Heck unfastened the hammer loop over his Colt. "I was told I might find a mountain man around here."

Plank nodded. "No better place to meet a mountain man this side of the Rockies. Most of them already headed west, but some are still lingering." Plank smiled. "If I'm not mistaken, I smell old Aaron Hays still sitting outside."

That filthy, old guy is a mountain man? Heck thought, figuring he'd sooner set out alone than ride alongside a cackling rooster of a man like Hays.

Plank chuckled. "Hays doesn't look like much, and he's riper than a gut pile, but he knows his business. You looking to get into trapping?"

"I do want to buy some traps, sir, but what I'm really looking for is someone who knows the trail, somebody I can trust to help me catch up with the wagon trains."

Plank nodded. "You mean the trains that know what they're doing."

"Yes, sir."

"Ride with us, boy," one of the three customers said, coming up behind Heck. He was a big man with a long black beard that almost reached the pommel of the huge knife shoved through his thick leather belt.

"No, thank you," Heck said.

"Why not?" the man growled, taking a step forward.

"I don't trust you," Heck said matter-of-factly.

The man offered a smile that didn't reach his glittering eyes. "You can trust us, boy."

Heck shook his head. "I'm not the trusting type. Thanks anyway."

The man gave a dismissive wave. "Good luck on the trail." The other two men stared cagily at Heck, who figured he'd best get out of there sooner rather than later.

He could pick up traps and other supplies in Council Grove. If he hung around here long enough to buy anything, these three might leave, get out in front of him, and prepare an ambush.

"Mr. Plank, thank you for the information. I reckon I best be going now." With a nod, Heck turned and headed for the door.

The three men elbowed each other and whispered as he passed.

"What about the traps?" Plank called after him.

Heck just raised a hand and went through the door.

As soon as he stepped onto the porch, he was back in the cloud of stench emanating from the man in the rocker—presumably Aaron Hays.

"Well, if nothin' else, you're an efficient shopper," Hays chuckled. "You ain't been in there long enough for a cat to clean his tail, and here you come back out again, with nothing to show for your visit. What were ya, hunting for credit?"

"I gotta get on down the trail," Heck said with a wave. He hurried down the steps, unhitched Red and Burly, and mounted up.

As Heck turned toward the trail, he heard the trading post

door bang open and knew without looking that the three rough men were coming after him.

Heck made no sign of this knowledge but got underway.

Behind him, Hays called, “Keep your powder dry, sonny.”

CHAPTER 13

Half a mile down the road, Heck left the trail and galloped across a meadow and into a stand of pin oaks. Moving quickly, he led Red and Burly back to the river and tied them to some birches, well out of the way of the coming storm.

He pulled the Hawken and his scattergun, grabbed his saddlebags, and hurried back to the oaks, where he arranged his weapons, along with his shot and powder and ramrods, and lay prone on the ground behind a fallen oak, leveling the Hawken across its thick trunk.

A few seconds later, the three men from the store rode into view. Reaching the point where he'd left the road, they stopped. The skinny one with a smudge of dark whiskers pointed to where Heck's crossing had bent the tall grass.

Heck put his sights on the big one who'd spoken to him in the store. It would be easy to knock him out of his saddle from this distance—around 100 yards—but even though he pulled the first trigger, setting the hammer, he couldn't drop it. Not yet. That would be murder.

At this point, as unlikely as it seemed, the men might not be trying to rob him. They might just have a proposition. Though he doubted this was the case, he held his fire.

The men stared toward his position, talking among themselves. He knew that they knew he was here, so he figured he might as well call their bluff. No sense giving them more time to plan an attack.

"Just keep on riding," he called across the meadow. "I don't want to have to kill y'all."

The men responded with loud laughter, telling Heck his suspicions had been correct. Then things happened quickly.

The men broke apart and charged into the field.

Heck pulled the trigger, knocked the black-bearded bandit from his saddle, and set to reloading.

By the time the Hawken was ready, the men had flanked him, disappearing into the woods to his left and right.

Heck's mind raced. He couldn't see or hear the men but knew what they would do. They would move in slowly from opposite directions, meaning to catch him in a crossfire.

He thought about backing toward the river but didn't want to put his animals in danger. Besides, those skinny river birches back there wouldn't offer much cover.

If he stayed where he was, however, they would get in close on both sides and cut him to pieces. So he slung his shotgun over his shoulder, left his saddlebags where they lay, took the Hawken in both hands, and moved to the right, cutting an angle between the river and where he thought his enemy might be. He stuck to the oaks and moved as quietly as possible, going tree to tree, watching and listening, every fiber of his mind and body ready for action even though once again, he worked with his trademark calm.

Each time he paused, Heck scanned in all directions, knowing the robbers could come at him from any direction.

As he moved again, a gunshot barked to his right, and a stitch of fire raced across the side of his head. There was no wallop to it, no concussion, but he knew he'd come half an inch from death. Spotting the smoke bloom sixty yards off, he shouldered the Hawken and charged in that direction.

Halfway to the shooter, Heck took cover behind a big oak.

Had the shooter moved?

He saw nothing of the man and couldn't know.

But he knew the other man would be coming in from his left now. Meanwhile, hot blood was running out of Heck's hair and down his cheek from where the bullet had grazed him.

A second later, a gunshot erupted from his left.

Reflexively, Heck dropped, but no bullet hit him or the tree or even whooshed by overhead.

Then the forest filled with cackling laughter he'd heard before.

Was Aaron Hays with these robbers?

The stinky old mountain man hollered, "These old boys was trying to flank ye, sonny, but I took care of the scoundrel on this side. What d'ye say we treat that other'n the way he was fixing to do ye? I'll come in from over here and ye work your way over to his other side."

The final robber must not have liked the sounds of that because he took a wild shot in Heck's direction and charged from cover, sprinting toward the field.

Heck nailed him right between the shoulder blades. There wasn't even much twitch left in him.

Off to the left, Hays came strolling into view, whistling cheerily, his own plains rifle hung over one shoulder.

"Thanks for the help," Heck said as they both reached the dead man on the ground.

"Don't mention it." He held out a filthy hand. "Aaron Hays. But folks call me Rabbit Foot."

Heck shook the man's hand, no longer caring about the grime. "Hector Martin, Jr., but folks call me Heck. Good to meet you."

"Likewise, Heck. Them boys wasn't too smart. Came out of Plank's and stood there right on the porch, paying me no mind and telling what they was gonna do." He gave another rip of cackling laughter.

"Well, I'm glad you followed. But tell me something. How come, after I shot, you just strolled over here with your rifle slung up? What if that shot you heard was him hitting me?"

Rabbit Foot snorted at that notion. "Ye think after forty years in the wilderness, I don't know the sound of a Hawken, sonny? I knew it was ye who fired and knew ye'd taken him out, too, on account of I also know the *ker-thump* of a bullet hitting a man hard. And with these big .54s, ye ain't got to be too particular where ye hit. Look at the size of the hole ye put in him. Ye roll him over, it'll be big enough to stick your head inside and take a peek."

Heck laughed. "I'd rather not."

They did roll the man over, though, as they searched his corpse, which they left for the buzzards.

Neither this man nor the one Rabbit Foot had killed had

much more than a rifle, shot, and powder. But after they got Heck's animals and walked back out into the field and found the one with the bushy, black beard, they were surprised to find not only the man's rifle and the big knife but also a flintlock pistol and ten dollars in silver coins.

"You go ahead and keep the loot," Heck said, picking up on the mountain man's word for the things they took off the dead.

"Pshaw! That won't do, Heck. We'll split it down the middle. Partners always split the take fifty-fifty."

"Partners?"

"That's right, partners. Wasn't ye telling Eleazer ye needed the services of a mountain man?"

Heck couldn't help but laugh. "Yeah, but how did you know?"

Grinning, Rabbit Foot tapped a gnarled finger against a patch of greasy gray hair covering his ear. "Ye want to be a mountain man, ye gotta see like an eagle, smell like a bloodhound, and hear like a wolf. Ye do want to be a mountain man, don't ye?"

"No, I just need a mountain man to guide me over the trail until we meet up with some of the wagon trains further along."

Rabbit Foot made a face like he'd bitten into a rotten apple. "What fer? Whaddaya propose to do with those idjits, go build a town, foul things up?"

"I don't know," Heck said honestly. "I hadn't really thought it through. I just want to see the West."

"See the West? Ye join a wagon train, all ye see is the trash-strewn trail and whatever ugly little town they pop up in the wilderness. Give it ten years, and it'll be just like all those towns ye left behind. Ye come with me, I'll show ye the West, and I mean the real West."

Heck chewed on that for a second, a whole new realm of possibilities opening before him. He grinned, thinking of his ring name, *Mountain Man*.

"Now, here's the situation," Rabbit Foot said. "I so happen to be running low on capital, or I'd already be halfway to the Rockies. Ye got enough to stake me?"

Heck nodded.

"Well then, sonny. Let's ride on back to Plank's, get everything we need, and ride west together. I'll take ye to South Park and teach ye how to hunt and trap. I'll show ye the ways of the mountains and introduce ye to all kinds of Injuns. Most'll be friends or folks to trade with. Some'll try to kill ye, but I'll teach ye how to kill them first. You'll make a fortune, meet men like Kit Carson and Jim Bridger, and really see the West... before your wagon trains ruin it all. What d'ye say, sonny?" He stuck out his dirty hand again. "We got a deal?"

Heck realized he was still grinning. It was funny the way life worked. Rabbit Foot had just explained exactly what Heck had wanted, without even knowing it, all along... a grand Western adventure, tramping across the wild frontier, living off the land, and building up a big bankroll in the process.

Impulsively, he seized Rabbit Foot's hand and shook it firmly. "We got a deal."

CHAPTER 14

They pulled out of Plank's leading a whole team of pack ponies, most of them loaded down with tobacco, blankets, and beads.

Heck hadn't balked at the cost of the ponies, but he'd expected to weigh them down with provisions. He was starting to question the mountain man's sanity when Rabbit Foot explained, "Sonny, we'll hunt our food. Eatin' won't be a problem. This here load is fer tradin'. Ye give them Injuns a handful of pretty beads, they'll load ye down with beaver pelts and fur robes. You'll make a fortune… if ye live long enough to come back this way."

The plains opened before them, providing ample grass for the beasts and ample game for Heck and Rabbit Foot. They killed turkeys and deer, rabbits and sage hen, and Rabbit Foot showed Heck how to forage along the trail.

Despite Heck's initial impression of Rabbit Foot, the mountain man proved to be incredibly knowledgeable. At mealtimes, he talked non-stop, telling Heck about the country ahead and teaching him a good deal of Indian sign language and Chinook, the patched-together language trappers used to communicate with various tribes.

A trade jargon that combined words from English, French, and various Indian dialects, Chinook had a very simple grammatical system and only a few hundred words, so it was easy to learn, and Heck was confident when they finally met with Indians, he would be able to communicate with them—whether they wanted to swap words or hot lead.

So far, they'd only glimpsed Indians twice. Both times, a lone rider skylighted out of rifle range, watched them for a while, and rode off.

A short time after crossing Cow Creek, Heck saw his first buffalo. There was quite a herd of them grazing along the hilly horizon. Heck and Rabbit Foot rode off the trail a way, drawing closer to the herd as they traveled up the creek.

Heck was mesmerized by the sight of this sprawling herd of huge, shaggy animals grazing the long grasses as clouds passed lazily overhead, mottling the rolling plain with drifting shadows.

This, he thought, *this is the West.*

Once they were within three hundred yards of the gigantic animals, Heck dismounted and picked a small buffalo, judged the distance and likely drop, and fired his Hawken.

The wallop echoed back across the plain. The buffalo toppled and wallowed briefly, kicking and raising a cloud of dust. By the time the cloud had dissipated, the beast lay still upon the ground.

Heck felt a surge of happiness. He'd shot his first buffalo and gotten them fresh meat.

Rabbit Foot clapped him on the shoulder and complimented his shooting, and they rode over to gut, skin, and butcher the beast.

That night, they camped along the creek and dined on thick slices of roasted liver, buttery bone marrow, and the best part of the buffalo, its fatty hump.

"Wish we had us a bottle of good old Taos Lightning," Rabbit Foot proclaimed. "Old Peg-Leg Smith sure did brew spicy whiskey. And strong? It'd put some fur on ye. And make ye feel lightning struck, too."

That night, they heard wolves snarling and fighting over the gut pile and remaining meat a hundred yards distant. Heck was not afraid, not in his mind or heart, but apparently, his body harkened back through its ancestry to a time before walls and roofs, when men dwelled side by side with dangerous predators, because the hair at the back of his neck stood straight up at the sounds.

They were off the trail a bit, with plenty of grass and water, so they camped for a few days, using the time to preserve meat. At mealtime, Heck was glad he'd shot a smaller animal because the steaks were tender and flavorful.

Rabbit Foot explained how to make pemmican, but there were no berries this time of year, and the grizzled trapper liked his pemmican with blueberries or saskatoons or choke cherries, so instead, they gorged themselves on prime cuts and sliced much of the meat into thin strips, which they hung to dry.

Returning to the trail, they left Cow Creek and followed the Arkansas River northwest, neglecting the southern Cimarron

Route favored by those heading to Santa Fe, and aimed their horses, mule, and ponies toward Bent's Fort instead.

With each day, they saw more buffalo until the herds grew so massive that the men lost time trying to skirt them, Rabbit Foot warning Heck of the deadly stampedes. "Ye get stuck in a stampede, them big old bufflers'll grind ye to pemmican."

The land grew so flat they could see for miles across the sea of waving grasses, upon which now fed not only herds of buffalo and deer and antelope but also bands of wild horses that made Heck love the West even more.

One morning as they were crossing these beautiful plains, they spotted a sizeable group of Indians riding their way.

Heck lowered a hand to his sheathed Hawken, but Rabbit Foot told him to leave it and sit up straight. "Show neither fear nor fight. Ye pull that gun, we're dead men."

CHAPTER 15

"What tribe are they?" Heck asked.

"Kiowa, likely. Let me do the talking. Young folk don't talk unless invited to. Understand?"

Heck nodded.

"And don't go smiling," Rabbit Foot said.

Heck did as he was told, sitting there like he was carved out of stone even as the Indians, thirty-strong, rode up to them.

Having heard all the tales of scalping and torture, Heck felt sort of jumpy, but he didn't let his anxieties show.

He had never been close to an Indian before. The Kiowa warriors were wiry and athletic with very dark skin and proud, angular faces that looked incapable of smiling.

Back in the world of St. Louis and all points east, folks spoke of Indians as animal-brained savages, but the alert, intelligent eyes of these men instantly put the hatchet to any notion along those lines.

Almost at once, the tension broke. These warriors knew

Rabbit Foot, shook his hand then shook Heck's, greeting them without menace.

Heck watched and listened, piecing together the ensuing conversation of Chinook and sign language.

The warriors invited them back to the village, which was only a few miles away.

Entering the lush valley where tipis sprawled away beneath the riverside cottonwoods, Heck was amazed. Well over 1000 tipis occupied the valley. How many Indians lived in this encampment, then? Surely over 3000. Maybe twice that. Maybe even more.

Everywhere he looked, he spied horses. No wonder the Kiowa were such famous horsemen.

The warriors led them to the chief, a tall man named Three Hatchets, whom they gave a stack of blankets and a pouch of beads, the good ones from Venice.

Three Hatchets was pleased. He shook their hands and gave them fur robes and invited them to join him for a meal.

"This is a great honor," Rabbit Foot whispered as they dismounted and surrendered their animals to the Indians. "Grab our bowls and spoons. That's expected when ye eat with an Injun."

Heck did as he was told.

As they made their way to Three Hatchets' tipi, Rabbit Foot whispered rapidly to his young charge. "The chief's door flap is open, so we walk straight in. I enter first. We'll go to the right, understand? Ye go left, you'll be declaring yourself a woman. Ye remember the sign for sit down?"

Heck nodded, held his fist to his chest, and made a stamping motion.

"That's right. We get in there, we wait for the chief to tell us where to sit. Sit cross-legged and eat whatever they give ye. All of it. Never walk between the fire and someone else. That's bad manners amongst these people. If all goes well, the chief'll invite us to a peace smoke."

Heck nodded. He'd heard of peace pipes.

Slowing as they reached the tipi, Rabbit Foot said, "When Three Hatchets knocks out his pipe and starts cleaning it, that means it's time for us to vamoose."

They went inside, and a dozen warriors joined them. Three Hatchets and Rabbit Foot did most of the talking. Heck and the others ate in silence, listening and watching as the two men, obviously old friends, talked about the previous winter, the buffalo herd, and the Kiowa's ongoing war with the Cheyenne.

It was a strange moment for Heck, all the stranger because everything felt so normal. Here he was, sitting among the "red devils" that raped, murdered, and mutilated white folks in the stories he'd heard back in the East. And these were Kiowa, the most populous tribe on the plains… and in those harrowing stories Heck had heard.

Yet here they all were, eating peacefully together. There was no menace, and yet he still believed those stories and knew these men with whom he ate were capable of terrible things.

At one point, Three Hatchets asked Heck how old he was.

Heck told him and said no more.

"He is tall," Three Hatchets remarked to Rabbit Foot, and that was the end of the conversation concerning Heck, which suited him just fine.

A short time later, two women entered, carrying a large silver platter bearing a boiled creature of medium size. Anticipation rippled through the tipi, the Kiowa perking up at the sight and savory smell of whatever meat this was.

Meanwhile, Heck was distracted by the platter itself. Fine scrollwork decorated its scalloped silver edges, telling him this was the work of white craftsmen back East.

Perhaps the Kiowa had traded for the platter.

But Heck doubted it.

A strange moment, indeed.

The unidentified meat was strange, too. Not bad, but unlike anything Heck had ever tasted. Slightly sweet, like a young woodchuck, but different. Judging by the shape and size, he wondered if it was a bear cub.

After supper, Three Hatchets invited them to share in a solemn peace smoke, a very good sign despite the lack of smiling. When the chief tapped out his pipe and started to clean it, Rabbit Foot, Heck, and the others left his tipi.

The Kiowa insisted they spend the night, so Rabbit Foot and Heck stayed, knowing to refuse would mean offending their hosts.

As they were bedding down, Heck asked, "That meat we had, was it bear cub?"

Rabbit Foot chuckled. "Nope. The Kiowa won't eat bear meat. It's taboo."

"What was it, then?"

Rabbit Foot's grin looked somehow ghoulish in the flickering light of the dwindling campfire. "I'd tell ye, but I don't want ye stinking up the tipi with your puke."

Heck conjured the image of the thing spread across the silver platter. It definitely hadn't been human. That was all that really mattered. "Tell me. I won't puke."

"Sonny," Rabbit Foot said, "the Kiowa just honored ye with their greatest delicacy."

Somehow, Heck managed not to puke when Rabbit Foot told him what they had eaten. But when they rode out of camp the next morning, parting with the Kiowa as friends, he felt sick all over again just thinking about it. "I hope that's the last time we're ever guests of honor in a Kiowa tipi," Heck said.

Rabbit Foot shrugged, grinning again. "Ain't so bad, once ye get used to the notion. Ye want to make it as a mountain man, you're gonna eat things that'd make a Billy goat puke. Besides, eating a dog now and then beats getting scalped."

THEY CONTINUED ALONG THE MOUNTAIN ROUTE OF THE SANTA Fe Trail, stopping to visit the Comanche on the way but dodging Cheyenne riders as they followed the Arkansas to Bent's Fort.

Here, Rabbit Foot introduced Heck to William Bent, one of the men who'd built the fort. Another of the builders, his brother Charles Bent, had been killed and scalped the previous year in the Taos Uprising.

Despite its name, Bent's Fort had been intended as a trading post, not a military fort. Ever since Kearney's Army of the West had marched into the war with Mexico, however, the fort had served as both a trading post and a military garrison. Here, Bent and the others bought and traded with white men and Indians alike, buying furs and robes to ship east.

For the next couple of weeks, they ventured out only to

hunt buffalo and trade with Indians, mostly Arapaho and Southern Cheyenne.

In trade, they gained many furs, which they sold to Mr. Bent for a good price, making a small fortune on their investment.

Other trappers drifted into the fort to stock up on last-minute provisions, too. Rabbit Foot introduced Heck to a compact, bowlegged, middle-aged man, short of stature but broad of shoulder and thick through the chest, with glittering, intelligent blue eyes and a confident smile splitting a blond goatee streaked with a few shimmering silver whiskers.

"Heck," Rabbit Foot said, "this here's the famous Kit Carson."

Heck smiled. He'd heard many stories about the great mountain man, scout, and hunter.

"Pleasure to meet you, my boy," Carson said, seizing Heck by the hand. "You certainly are a tall'un."

Carson introduced Heck to his assistant, Mr. Hughes, and Carson's sixteen-year-old nephew, Will Drannan, whom Heck liked very much.

Over the next few weeks as they geared up for the trip into the mountains, Heck spent a lot of time with Will Drannan, who had been on the frontier for only a year but was full of amazing stories. Heck wasn't sure he believed everything the boy said, but he sure did tell some exciting stories.

Of course, at this point, Heck had no idea that he would come out of the mountains packing a similar bounty of wild stories and life-changing experiences and that two years later, his life back East would seem as soft and simple as a summer dream.

CHAPTER 16

Two years later...

The soldiers at the gate made way as the towering, muscular man in filthy buckskins strode into Bent's Fort. His great height, powerful physique, and black beard all conspired to hide his youth, but what disguised his age even more effectively were his absolute confidence, hard blue eyes, and the panther-like fluidity of his every movement.

Though few would have guessed he was only seventeen years old, no one at Bent's Fort would have mistaken his identity.

For over the course of the last two years, Heck Martin had become a famous mountain man, trapper, scout, hunter, and Indian fighter.

He and Rabbit Foot had made a fortune trapping beaver in the mountains, and Heck had taken two dozen scalps, mostly Ute, out there in the wilds. Most of these warriors he'd killed with the Hawken, with which he had become a legendary shot, but he had also finished men with knives, split skulls with his tomahawk, and snapped one Ute's neck with his bare hands.

Among the native peoples of the mountains, Heck had become something of a boogeyman. They called him *Puck-ki Qua-ab* or Killing Oak for his deadliness, strength, and great height.

At six feet, five inches tall, Heck was nearly a foot taller than most men. But he was no longer the skinny boy who'd set off into the mountains with Rabbit Foot. He remained lean, but his shoulders had broadened, and his entire body rippled with iron muscles. Around the iron muscles cording his neck, he still wore his dear mother's wedding band on the leather string.

Despite his formidable physique and reputation as a killer of men, Heck had also become a great friend to many tribes, much like his predecessors Rabbit Foot, Kit Carson, and Jim Bridger.

Between trapping adventures, he hunted for the soldiers at Bent's Fort and served as a scout for the cavalry. The best part of working alongside the soldiers was getting to know the officers, who allowed Heck to borrow from the impressive library of titles the Army of the West had carted to the fort. Heck's mind was ravenous, and he devoured everything from novels to plays to scientific texts to books on military history, strategy, and tactics.

This, in turn, delighted the officers, a few of whom enjoyed talking books with Heck the way a man might enjoy taming a wild wolf with nightly feedings of raw meat.

Though, of course, a wolf can never really be tamed, no matter how many bloody steaks you toss it; and Heck, despite his voracious appetite for learning, could never really be fully civilized. He continued to live life nose to ground, brightly alive in a hard world that took few prisoners and tendered no apologies.

Captain Avery Scottsdale, a West Point man fascinated by this towering, well-read savage, shook Heck's hand upon arrival.

"Where's your partner?" Scottsdale asked, seeing Rabbit Foot nowhere in sight.

"Taos."

"Taos? I expected he'd be heading out to trap with you again. Is he injured?"

Heck shook his head. "He got married."

"Married?" Scottsdale laughed. "What kind of woman would let a man who smells like that into her bed?"

"One who makes him bathe regularly," Heck said.

Rabbit Foot and Juana had met at a fandango and were happy together.

Half Mexican, half Apache, and not much older than Heck, Juana was a plump little thing with bright eyes and a soft voice. She reminded Heck of a quail.

Rabbit Foot doted on her. He built her a house and even hired some of the girls who used to mock her as a half-breed.

Heck was happy for the newlyweds.

"Well, this news comes as a surprise, but good for them. I have to ask, Heck, what are you planning to do?"

Heck shrugged. "I'm trying to figure that out now. You seen Kit around?"

"No," Scottsdale said, and his smile returned. "I hear he

settled down, too. Makes one wonder if there's something in the water out there."

"What about Bridger?"

Scottsdale shook his head. "Bridger's gone. Heard he married that Shoshone caretaker of his and they've gone back to Missouri. Got himself a few hundred acres to farm."

"Jim Bridger, a farmer?"

"The wonders never cease," Scottsdale said. "Were you thinking of working with him?"

Again, Heck shrugged. Truth be told, he had no idea what he wanted to do. He wouldn't mind working alongside Bridger, especially if the famous trailblazer was going to be traveling long distances. No one knew the country better, and Heck could learn a lot.

But Heck didn't feel like trapping another season. He was at loose ends with himself, uncharacteristically restless, like a wild beast hearing the first, faint call of a migratory instinct.

Yes, he could make a good deal of money if he went trapping again, but what of it? He already had over $15,000, enough money to kick back wherever he liked and never work again.

Which sounded like death to him.

He knew he had to keep moving, keep exploring, but he just didn't know where he was supposed to go or who he was supposed to throw in with when he got there.

"Why not enlist?" Captain Scottsdale said. "We could use a man like you."

Heck shook his head. "I'm not much for following orders."

Scottsdale laughed at that. "No, I shouldn't suppose you would be. Will you head east?"

"Not a chance," Heck said.

"Hey, Heck!" a boy's voice called, and Heck saw young Casey come running out of the trading post, apron fluttering, waving a white envelope overhead. "You got a letter, Heck. Been holding it for you for months!"

Heck felt a jolt of surprise. He hadn't received a letter since leaving St. Louis what seemed like a thousand years earlier. He had written the Mullens a letter and explained his rough plans prior to leaving Plank's post back on the Missouri and upon Rabbit Foot's advice had mentioned Bent's Fort, but he had never expected to hear from them here—or anywhere, truth be told.

His heart sped up like it hadn't in many a month as Casey handed him the envelope and Heck saw the elegant handwriting of Mrs. Mullen on the outside of the envelope.

"Thank you," Heck said, and tipped the boy a whole dime before retreating to one wall, where he leaned back, jacked up one boot behind him, and used the tip of his skinning knife to open the envelope.

He returned the knife to its sheathe and unfolded the letter, forcing himself to move slowly and deliberately, having long ago recognized haste as a weakness no man could afford on the frontier.

But he was excited. More excited than he'd been in a long, long time.

The date atop the letter gave him pause. Mrs. Mullen had written four months ago.

Would the Mullens assume he had ignored them? That he hadn't cared enough to respond?

How he hoped that wasn't the case. He'd sooner they thought he was dead than ambivalent.

As his eyes whipped across the neat handwriting, Heck's heart seemed to ride the swell and dip of every letter.

Mrs. Mullen had written to let Heck know they had finally sold the farm and were heading west on the Oregon Trail.

This filled him with both joy and trepidation. If only he had known sooner, he would have raced across the country to escort them safely to their destination.

But it was too late for that now. They would already be a good deal of the way across the trail unless something had happened to them along the way.

He hated to consider the dangers they would be facing.

But he did consider them and decided he would help the Mullens any way he could.

Reaching the bottom of the letter, he saw Hope's beautiful handwriting in the postscript.

P.S. I do so hope we can be reunited in the West, Heck.

Was it possible that Hope still loved him? Was that what she had meant? Or was that just wishful thinking on his part? Was she just being polite?

He didn't know, couldn't know, but he was determined to find out and to help the Mullens regardless of Hope's feelings for him.

Suddenly, he understood why he had been so restless and knew exactly what he wanted to do.

But the Mullens had probably been on the trail for several weeks. Where would that put them?

He had no clue but knew someone who could tell him. Rabbit Foot had ridden the trail half a dozen times, and the map of the land between here and there was written in his mind and on his heart.

Looked like Heck was bound for Taos. But he'd have to hurry.

The Mullens needed him. Hope needed him.

Heck only hoped they would be safe until he could intercept them. What dangers were they facing on the long and arduous trail west?

CHAPTER 17

"Do you think they will attack?" Hope asked, looking out across the rolling sameness in the direction her father and brother and two scouts had ridden off, hunting for signs of the murderous bandits.

"I cannot say, Hope," her mother said. Her face was drawn and dirty thanks to the rigors of the trail and the dust rolling up from the oxen.

First mud, now dust. The trail was never easy. She could only hope that Oregon lived up to the promises that had beckoned them.

Whatever the case and whatever the conditions, Hope hated seeing her mother's face in such a state. It made her look old and tired, like a glimpse into some unhappy future.

But her mother's voice was as calm as ever, and her words were just as strong as the day they'd left the farm all those weeks ago.

"What I can say, Hope, is that God has blessed us. Despite

the many challenges of this voyage, He has surely shielded us to this point. Yes, folks have died, but the good Lord has shielded us from bandits and Indians so far, and for that I am very grateful."

"So you believe He will continue to shield us, Mother?" Even as the words left her mouth, Hope knew this wasn't what her mother was saying, but she couldn't help herself. The horrific things they'd discovered that morning had unnerved her.

"I have no way of knowing," her mother said, "but the good Lord has shown us favor to this point. I do not claim or even suspect that He will see us through unscathed. Whatever the case, we must remain vigilant as we go about the business of our days. That's all we have: one day, followed, hopefully, by another. And the concerns of each are sufficient. So… what do you think you should be doing now?"

Hope reached under the seat and grabbed the burlap sack. "Gathering fuel, Mother."

"That is correct."

"Yes, Mother," Hope said, and inched her way to the side. "I will do that now."

But her mother stopped her. "Hope, wait. I don't mean to dismiss you, dear. I wish you hadn't seen those things this morning. I truly do. I wish none of us had seen them, and I know that I will continue seeing those terrible things in nightmares for years to come. But a part of me is also grateful for the experience."

"Grateful?"

"Yes, because we are decent people, Hope. And the people with us are, by and large, decent people, as were our neighbors back in Kentucky; as, I hope, our new neighbors in Oregon will be."

Hope nodded. Much like her father, she had always had an adventurous spirit, but her time on the trail had revealed something else to her. More than anything, she wanted to return to what they'd left.

Not Kentucky, exactly, not the farm they'd sold. But that sort of life. A life of stability and tranquility, a life where a girl was free to dream of adventure without having to worry about the various and endless trials of the trail, let alone the tragic scene they had discovered that morning.

"But between here and Oregon," her mother continued, "we must never forget that there are rough people in the world, people as cursed as the Canaanites from the Old Testament, as wicked as the generations that caused God to flood the Earth. Do you understand what I'm saying?"

"Yes, ma'am."

"We've known all along that these sorts were out here. That's why every wagon carries a rifle and why we hired scouts and post guards and keep an eye on the horizon. But knowing is one thing..."

"And seeing is another," Hope finished for her.

"Yes, dear. Seeing and smelling both."

Hope nodded then swallowed with difficulty, remembering the terrible smells of the atrocity.

"The wicked are afoot, Hope. And you know what they would like to do to us, to your father and brother, to everyone. I pray the Lord Jesus will see us safely through, but meanwhile, we must remember what we saw, what these evil men did to folks like us, folks who no doubt also prayed for deliverance, perhaps even with their dying breaths. We must keep a sharp eye and keep our weapons close by." She patted the shotgun beside her. "Yes?"

"Yes, ma'am."

"You sweet girl," her mother said, reaching out to caress Hope's face. "You poor, sweet child. One day, this will all be over."

Hope nodded. "Yes, ma'am."

"Has Basil been giving you any trouble?"

Hope shook her head. "Not really."

"Well, if he does, you let me know. Your father will speak with him."

"Thanks, Mother."

Her mother smiled, and for a brief moment, she no longer looked quite so old or tired.

It made Hope smile in return. She hopped down from the wagon with her sack. "Back to my glorious adventure on the frontier."

Her mother laughed as Hope walked to the back of the wagon and started gathering chips from the badly rutted ground.

This year, the trail had seen a tremendous number of emigrants. Good grass was harder to find near the trail, which had widened to half a mile at some points, and the game had all but dried up. Every wagon had been forced to cut more deeply into their food supplies than expected.

And yet, Hope marveled as she filled her sack with the dried manure of oxen who'd already passed this way, she was always hungry.

Always, always, always.

She'd lost weight, too. She'd always been a lean girl, but now her ribs were like a washboard.

She had not lost her womanly curves, however. Normally, this would have been a good thing. But with Basil in the train, it made things difficult.

Once the sack was full, she poured it into the canvas fuel hammock nailed underneath the wagon. Then she started picking up more manure.

The work didn't bother her. She had never minded getting her hands dirty. Nor had she minded mucking stalls. She hadn't even minded blood overmuch.

What bothered her now, however, was never being able to get clean.

That was another thing she had learned about herself on the trail. Getting dirty was one thing, a state she associated with pleasurable things like working the farm and riding Dolly, but never being able to get clean was something altogether different.

Day after day, she perspired in the heat, and the dirt and dust and bits of grass clung to every inch of her. She felt filthy and grimy and wanted more than anything to just sink into a warm bath and scrub herself clean.

Don't be foolish, she scolded herself, dropping another crumbly chip into her sack. *None of that matters. Not now. Not until we reach safety.*

And once again, her mind filled with the terrible things she'd seen this morning.

Bandits had hit a small wagon train at night while they had stopped for camp. They'd killed everyone. The men, the women, even the children.

One of the men had been stripped naked and tortured. She wouldn't think about that.

Mr. Devereux, the wagon master, said the bandits had done that to throw folks off the trail, to make them think Indians had done it. He said that's why they'd left an arrow, too.

But the real damage had been done with firearms, and they'd ridden upon shod horses and made no attempt at covering their tracks coming or going.

The bandits had done things to the older girls and women before killing them, too. She also wouldn't think about that.

Or at least she would try not to think about those things.

"Hey, Hope," Willa said, catching up with her.

"Hi, Willa. Are you feeling better?"

Willa smiled weakly. "Somewhat."

The sweet girl had reacted poorly to the massacre scene. Hope had reacted poorly, too, but mostly, she'd contained the horror within herself.

Willa, who was seventeen like Hope, had screamed and vomited and hidden herself away in her family's wagon.

She still looked a little pale beneath the dust covering her pretty face.

Willa had brought a sack of her own. They gathered fuel together, talking idly, first of the bandits then of train gossip. Willa reported that Mrs. Singleton, sporting a black eye, had abandoned her husband and moved into the Wilsons' wagon.

Finally, Willa got around to her favorite subject: young men.

"I wish Heck was here," Hope confessed.

"Is that the boy who ran off to the mountains?"

"The *man*. Even at fourteen, Heck wasn't really a boy. He was a man."

Willa bounced her dark eyebrows. “Mmm. Tell me more.”

Even though she knew it was ridiculous, Hope felt a twinge of jealousy at Willa’s interest in Heck. “We loved each other at first sight. That’s all that matters.”

“Well, it sounds to me like he’s long gone. I don’t mean to be cruel, Hope. I really don’t. But why cling to a ghost when you have a fine young man pining for your affections? If I were you—”

“You’d throw your arms around Basil’s neck and give him a big kiss.”

Willa tittered and pinkened but didn’t deny it. “Well, yes. He’s so handsome and well-formed and educated. Not to mention wealthy. Father says Basil’s going to be a great man in Oregon. He certainly sits a horse well, doesn’t he?”

Hope nodded. “He does. And he’s well aware of that fact. Question is, if he’s so strong and such a great horseman, why isn’t he out with the scouts, looking for those bandits?”

Willa shrugged. “He sent his hired men.”

Hope shivered. “Those two gunmen of his frighten me.”

“Pearson and Clark can be quite crude,” Willa agreed. “Why just the other day—”

“Good afternoon, ladies,” a deep voice called, and they turned to see Basil Paisley marching toward them from the front of the column.

As usual, Basil wore remarkably clean clothing that looked ridiculous on the frontier. Just how many outfits had he carted into the wilderness?

Many, clearly, which wasn’t a problem thanks to the wealth and many wagons of Basil’s father, who planned on establishing a business empire in the West.

"Good morning, Basil!" Willa called, waving at the approaching young man.

Basil was tall—nearly six feet, Hope would guess—and well-built with a handsome face anchored by a big, lantern jaw and topped by a curly mane of glossy black hair, which dropped all the way to the collar of his neatly tailored shirt.

Yes, he was physically impressive, but he was loud and conceited, and Hope had never seen him do any actual work since they'd left Missouri.

Hope neither liked nor trusted Basil, and she wished he would leave her alone.

She'd told him as much, but he wouldn't take no for an answer, which made him even more repulsive to her.

As Basil approached, Hope picked up another piece of manure, figuring she would rather speak with it than this self-important, would-be suitor.

"Ladies, please," Basil said, strutting over to them like a peacock in broadcloth. "That work is beneath you. Stop at once, and I'll send someone to do the work for you."

"Thanks so much, Basil!" Willa chimed.

Hope, on the other hand, responded by picking up another chip. "I'm not above work," she said, "and I hope I never am."

"Dear Hope, you don't know your own worth," Basil said. "Willa, would you give Hope and me a minute alone, please?"

"Sure, Basil. I should be getting back to Mother anyway. She'll be wanting help with the baby. Goodbye, Basil. Bye, Hope."

As Willa walked off, Basil looked Hope up and down. It made her feel like she was crawling with ticks. "Have you been avoiding me, Hope?"

"Yes."

"Why?"

"Because I don't want to see you."

"You just don't know me. And you don't understand life yet."

She snorted at that but said nothing.

"Have you considered my offer, Hope?"

"I already told you no."

"Have you reconsidered?"

"I don't need to reconsider. I told you no. That was my answer, is my answer, and will always be my answer. I don't mean to be rude, Basil, but as I've already explained, my heart belongs to another."

"Some nobody who ran off into the wilderness."

"Heck Martin is not a nobody," she said, anger rising in her. "He's the finest young man I've ever met in my entire life."

Basil chuckled as if she'd told a joke. "Look, Hope. You see all those wagons up there, all those cows, all those servants? Those belong to my family. And since I'm Father's oldest son, one day they will all belong to me. And that's just the start of it. Father has businesses and bank accounts back east that—"

"I don't care," Hope said, stuffing oxen chips into the bag with a vengeance. "I told you already. I don't care about your name or your money or any of it, and nothing you can say will change my mind."

Basil seized her by the arm and jerked her to a stop so forcefully that she dropped her sack. His eyes flashed with savage lust and the hot anger of a spoiled child not getting his way. "Don't talk to me that way, Hope. You will be mine."

Hope tugged at her arm, but it was no use. Basil was very strong. "Please unhand me, Basil."

"No."

"You're hurting me."

"I'm getting impatient with you, Hope," he growled.

"Let go of her right now, boy, or you'll spend the rest of your life wishing you had."

"Daddy!" Hope cried with relief.

Basil released her arm and stepped back, eyeing Tom Mullen warily.

Hope's father stepped between them. He was much smaller than Basil but much fiercer, too. "I don't care who you are, boy. You touch my daughter again, and I'll hit you so hard with the left, you'll beg for the right. D'ya'understand, boy?"

Basil showed his palms and took a few steps back, clearly frightened, despite his advantage in size and youth. "I was merely—"

"Get out of here," Hope's father snapped. "One more word out of you, and—"

He didn't need to finish because Basil was already trotting off like a beaten rooster with a drooping comb.

"Are you okay, my dear?" her father asked.

"Yes, Daddy. We just had a misunderstanding is all. Thank you for clearing that up. I'm sure he'll leave me alone now."

Which was a lie, of course. She didn't really believe that. In fact, she'd bet their whole wagon and everything in it that Basil would be back within a few days.

But she didn't want her father to worry and especially didn't want him to get forceful, because Basil's father owned half the wagon train and had hired the wagon master and, by extension, the scouts.

If her father actually hit Basil, what would they do to him?

That was a risk she couldn't take, so she quickly switched the subject. "Did you find any signs of the bandits?"

Her father stooped to pick up a piece of dried ox manure, dropped it in the sack, and nodded grimly. "I'm afraid so, my love. We'll need to be awfully careful at the next river crossing."

CHAPTER 18

Heck switched horses every couple of hours and had packed Burly lightly, so they made good time sticking mostly to creeks and rivers.

This territory was not as beautiful as much of the ground he'd covered between here and Taos, but it was nonetheless gorgeous country, and there was a fierce starkness that appealed to Heck. Despite the heat of the day, a cool and ceaseless wind blew down out of the mountains, bearing a strange sharpness unlike anything one might ever smell in the lowlands. This was a land of sand and cliff, of jagged peaks bearded in ponderosa, and that ceaseless wind from on high, as pure and cold as water from a glacier-fed stream.

The trip had taken him only three weeks, a pleasant surprise given the unfamiliar, mountainous terrain and the time of year, which meant the tribes were out on the trail, riding and raiding.

He'd had only one brush with Indians the entire way, and

that had come on his second day, when he'd failed to outrun a trio of Utes.

Ultimately, they were left wishing that he had outrun them. Or rather, their families were left wishing. The three Utes themselves were dead.

Now, having reached the trail and backtracked on the stream to the exact point Rabbit Foot had described, Heck saw the work of a far more successful raiding party.

Unfortunately, the moldering dead slumped against the cabin were none other than Rabbit Foot's friend and fellow mountain man, Badger Yates, and what Heck guessed as Yates's squaw.

It was hard to say for sure, of course. Between weather, animals, and bugs, the pair had been reduced to rags and bones. But given their mode of dress, the location of the cabin, and the amazing property surrounding their home, Heck was confident it was them.

The cabin was situated on a beautiful bench just above the high-water mark. The plot enjoyed a southern exposure and the surrounding mountains rose on both sides to block the wind but not the sun or rain, creating a fertile bottomland, a dozen or so acres of which Badger and his squaw had planted with corn and wheat and vegetables. The corn was knee-high already and green as a summer dream.

Having grown up on a farm, Heck hated to see the neglected crop almost as much as the arrow-riddled heaps of bone and clothing slumped against the thick cabin timbers.

Who had done this?

Early spring raiders, obviously. But what tribe?

He was probably too far north for Utes. He doubted it was

Shoshones. This was their territory, but they tended to be friendly with whites.

Likely, it had been the Cheyenne, the Sioux, or a band of south-riding Crows.

Animals had torn the buckskins and strewn the bones of the mountain man and his squaw.

The empty sockets of Badger's skull stared up at the vast blue sky. The jaw hung wide open, as if the mountain man was laughing at his own death.

Heck crouched before the skull. "Rabbit Foot says hello. Wish you coulda been alive to hear that. Looks like you had a nice place here."

Heck lifted his eyes and scanned the area. He saw nothing, heard nothing, smelled nothing.

But he felt something.

It felt like he was being watched.

He waited, watching and listening and sniffing the air, but all that came to him was the wind rustling the leaves and the faint odor of old decay.

Inwardly, he shrugged. Places like this often felt strange, he knew. As they should, what with the unburied dead strewn atop the ground.

He stood and studied the place.

There were no fresh tracks anywhere, no sign of anyone coming or going.

The large vegetable garden and planted fields were positioned at a bend in the stream after a stonewalled canyon, so spring floods would deposit rich soil all along the bottomland, creating unusually fertile land for this region. Which explained why, despite the tall weeds, the garden was doing so well.

The cabin was built into the stony slope and looked very strong with two loopholes staring out from a face of heavy timbers.

Seventy or eighty feet away, a corral fronted a stable that was also built into the mountainside.

Heck led his mule and horses into the corral and took off their packs and saddles and let them crop the tall grasses. There was even a narrow, gurgling stream cutting through the corral.

Rabbit Foot hadn't been kidding. Badger had created a little slice of heaven here.

At least until the devils found him.

Heck entered the cabin. Within, the air was close. He crouched, swiveling half out of the doorway to let the sunlight fall into the cabin, and studied the dusty floor. Other than the marks of a few mice, he found no tracks.

Within, the raiders had ransacked the place, overturning furniture and carrying off anything of real value to them.

Which came as no surprise.

What did come as a surprise was the size of the cabin. Badger had floored the main area, a space twenty feet wide and thirty deep.

Though the raiders had carried off most of the mountain man's possessions, they had left much behind, including flour and salt, plates and bowls, and a variety of vegetable seeds that Badger had no doubt been meaning to plant later in the season.

Beyond the main cabin, the space under the rim became a cave, creating a natural corridor wide and high enough for a draft horse to pass.

Heck retrieved a lamp from the wall, pulled matches from his buckskins, and lit the wick.

By its flickering light, he navigated the cave, which forked, two corridors of similar size heading off in different directions, one to the left, one straight ahead into the mountain.

He went straight first, following the faint sound of running water.

Twenty feet back, he discovered a short door of wooden planks leaned against the wall. Hauling it aside, he was struck by the smell of potatoes brightened by the aroma of ripe apples. He peered inside and saw a cavern that had been converted into a root cellar.

Descending a set of wooden stairs, he marveled at the hidden treasure: hundreds of bushels of potatoes; a similar number of apples; a mountain of squash; and two mountains of dried corn. Further back hung what looked like enough smoked meat to feed three or four families through a hard winter.

Heck walked around the meat and stopped to stare at what looked like a smoked ham.

Much of it was missing.

It hadn't been hacked away by teeth. It had been sliced away.

And many of those slices had been peeled away recently.

He crouched and studied the cave floor. At first, his examination only increased the mystery. There was no sign of anyone having passed.

Then, studying one patch more carefully, he found the brush marks.

Someone had passed here recently. And they had gone to some trouble trying to cover their tracks.

Knowing what he was looking for, he followed the brushed-away tracks to a pile of stones against one shadowy cave wall.

Examining these, he could see that some of the rocks were

dustier than others. The three larger stones at the center had been moved, leaving subtle scrape marks along the floor.

Heck pulled these stones aside and discovered a passageway that plunged away into darkness. It was wide enough for a child or woman or a small man, but a man of his size couldn't do much more than stick his head inside.

Which he was smart enough not to do, thank you very much.

That would be a good way to get shot.

Who had been using this place?

"If you can hear me," he called into the passage, "my name's Heck Martin, and I mean you no harm."

There was no response.

Heck shoved two potatoes in his pockets. The room was cool and dry, and he smelled no rot, only the musty smell of stored potatoes.

Then, snatching up an apple, he left the room and closed the door behind him.

Further on, the corridor led to massive, high-vaulted cavern across the center of which a shallow, fast-running stream had cut a groove in the smooth stone.

Heck chuckled at the perfection of this place. Not just shelter but all the food and water a family could want.

Such a shame about Badger and his squaw.

But then again, what had happened to them was just as much a part of this wild frontier as freedom or shiny golden nuggets or the promise of prime land for the taking.

He scanned the large room quickly, not wanting to spend much longer investigating. After all, whoever had used that tiny corridor in the root cellar might very well still be somewhere close, might even be riding off on Red right now.

Though he doubted that. Red was a one-man stallion. It would take one heck of a cowboy to stay on top of him.

Still, it wouldn't do to tarry.

So he backtracked to the fork and headed out the other passage, figuring he knew where it would lead him.

Sure enough, it led straight to the stable, which was actually a huge chamber portioned into two vast spaces.

The front room extended back from the wooden stable face, a space large enough to comfortably house a dozen horses or more.

A high wooden fence complete with a gate ran across the back of this space, separating it from the other half of the chamber, where a mountain of tinder-dry hay towered beside hills of richer feed: dried corn and dozens of sacks of grain.

Amazing.

What had Badger wanted with all this bountiful feed and supplies?

Maybe he'd just been a careful type, stocking up in case he got hurt or killed. Perhaps, like many mountain men, he'd been planning on taking a few more wives and filling the place with children. Or maybe—and Heck suspected this to be the most likely guess—old Badger had been planning on setting up shop and trading with folks who passed on the trail.

Whatever the case, it was all for naught. Badger was gone, along with his squaw, his dreams, and whatever livestock he'd been keeping here... horses and cows and pigs, judging by the look of the dried dung.

The raiders had taken them, no doubt.

Question was, why hadn't they burned this place?

Perhaps, they, too, had marveled over Badger's dwelling and supplies. Perhaps they had spared it thinking they might return someday. Or perhaps, as some tribes did, they had spared this place out of respect for the man who'd died trying to defend it.

Heck forked some hay onto the stable floor then poured out scoops of grain and opened the big door and called his horses and mule inside.

"Welcome to the Cavern Restaurant, boys," he said as they nosed the grain. "Tonight's special is the best feed you've had since leaving Fort Bent."

Then he took a pick and shovel from the wall and went back outside, where he again addressed the dead.

"Yeah, quite a place you had here. Really something." He shook his head. "You deserved better than this. At the very least, I can help you rest in peace."

He moved off a short distance and started digging. The topsoil was deep and dark. Having grown up farming the thin, rocky soil of the Kentucky mountains, Heck couldn't help but feel a thrill, digging two feet into the black-dark soil without hitting a single stone.

When he finally struck a rock, he worked the blade of the shovel around its edge, slid deeper, and easily levered the stone free.

As he was bending to retrieve it, his senses sharpened, brought to full life by a faint smell, or rather, smells: perspiration and fear.

As these things registered, he heard the metallic click of a shotgun hammer behind him and knew someone had him dead to rights.

CHAPTER 19

By the late spring of 1850, the Oregon Trail was an enormous, horribly rutted roadway, wide enough in some places to build a town upon its surface. But in certain other spots, such as river crossings, the trail narrowed again, the rivers proving downright stubborn in their refusal to ease the struggles of the westward way.

Heavy rain overnight had muddied the banks and swollen the river, but the wagon master, Mr. Devereux, declared it crossable, and now, half the train had made it safely to the other side.

Hope and Tom were among them. Sitting atop their horses, they watched with hammering hearts as their parents drove the wagon into the swirling, muddy current.

Meanwhile, the front of the train was already moving forward again. Always onward, always westward. Every minute of every hour counted on the trail. They had to reach Oregon in time to build shelter before the first snow fell.

"That wasn't so bad," Tom said, smiling beside her. He'd been worried about the rain.

"No, it wasn't," Hope agreed, glad she'd worn britches for the crossing. They were soaked now, of course, as were her riding boots. "Once I got Dolly to quit drinking and start crossing, it was easy."

"Why didn't you water her earlier?"

"I did!"

They laughed.

And then, as if mocking their laughter, the first shots rang out.

Men fired down on the train from a bluff upstream. A second later, several other men came streaming out from behind the bluff, firing pistols as they charged the lead wagons.

Hope watched them, frozen in terror, and saw the two lead riders with the clarity that so often arises in moments when life suddenly hangs in the balance.

One bandit was a large man—too large, it seemed, to ride a horse—though the horse beneath him was itself quite large. The other bandit was a black man in a faded pink shirt.

As she stared, the large man shot Barney Plott, the lead scout, from his saddle, and the black man shot Mr. Baker, the blacksmith, as Baker was running for cover.

But then Tom cried out beside her, pointing into the river, and Hope forgot all about these terrible men and the rest of the train.

Her father hunched atop his seat, holding the wagon reins in one hand. His other hand clutched his side. His shirt was dark with blood—so much blood!—and her mother was leaning over him, gripping his shoulders with a terrified expression on her face.

Beside Hope, Tom unslung his rifle, staring toward the bluff with bulging eyes. Then, seeing his sister move, he hollered, "Hope! What are you doing?"

"I have to help Daddy!" she cried, charging on Dolly back into the river.

Gunshots and screaming filled the air.

She fought against her terror, urging Dolly into the raging current.

But then the Cranstons' out-of-control wagon smashed into her family's wagon with a loud thump.

Her parents' schooner buckled, the terrified oxen jerked, and the strong current overturned the wagon.

Hope screamed as she watched her father fall face-first into the river and disappear.

Her mother surfaced at once and struggled out of the way of the wagon, which spun in the river, spilling their possessions and dragging the oxen, who had also tumbled into the current.

Hope's father was nowhere in sight.

With a cry of terror, Hope leapt from her horse and plunged into the current and swam downstream.

The muddy water churned violently, showing her nothing. She slammed into one rock, then another, crying out in pain but struggling ever forward, determined to save her father.

Where was he?

A bullet slapped the water beside her head.

She dove under the surface, banged off another rock, and saw a blur of color just downstream.

She swam for all she was worth, fighting against the weight

of her sodden clothes and boots, thankful now for all the times she had disobeyed her father and sneaked off to go swimming.

Seeing the blur again, she raced toward it, and—praise God! —saw it was, indeed, her father.

But no sooner had she filled with elation than fear once again gripped her heart in its icy claw; because as she reached her father, she saw by the limp tumbling of his body that he was either unconscious or…

Wrapping her arms around him, Hope swam to the surface. Holding him with one arm, she pulled with the other and kicked with her legs, swimming for shore but going with the current rather than against it, drifting steadily downstream as she drew closer to safety.

Upstream, the gunfire was dying out.

"Thank you, Jesus!" Hope cried as her fingers raked across rocks. Trembling with exhaustion, she dragged her father into the shallows.

Struggling for breath, hurting all over from the battering she'd taken, she stood on shaking legs and despite her exhaustion, lifted her father from the swallows and carried him to the western riverbank with all the strength of a mother grizzly defending a cub.

Only this wasn't a cub. This was her father, whom she loved more than life itself.

She laid him gently on the ground, horrified by the blood pouring from his side and the terrible gash just above his ear. Another gash had sliced him open just above one eyebrow, and his face was as slack and pale as death.

CHAPTER 20

Heck raised his hands.

"Frienderfoe?" a voice said behind him.

"Friend," Heck said, keeping his hands high as he twisted around and saw a filthy, half-Indian boy of eleven or twelve years holding a shotgun on him. The boy's eyes bulged with tension, but he held the scattergun steady.

"Whaddarye doin', mister?"

"Digging a grave for these good folks. This man, Badger, was a friend of a friend."

The boy relaxed a touch. "Who?"

"Rabbit Foot."

The boy tensed all over again. "An Injun?"

"No, a white man. A mountain man, just like Badger. They did some trapping together years back, down on the Arkansas."

The boy lowered the barrel. "Well, mister, you done got the name right, anyway. Badger Yates was the best mountain man who ever lived."

Heck nodded, considering the boy's dark hair and fierce loyalty to the dead man. "You his boy?"

The boy lifted his chin. "Yessir. I'm Badger's son, Seeker."

"Seeker, huh? Good name for a boy. I'm Heck."

"Heck?"

"Short for Hector. So you're the one who's been using the root cellar."

The boy nodded. "How'd you know?"

"Had to look awful close. You did a good job covering your tracks. And you haven't been around here at all, have you? The garden or stable or in the main cabin, I mean."

"Hardly any," the boy said, "other than to plant. Gotta get crops in the ground or I'll starve this winter."

"Your taters are holding up."

"Getting soft. Come winter, they'll set to rotting. I need new ones. But you can't do that."

"Do what?"

"You can't dig graves. Injuns come through sometimes. They see the dead been buried, they'll stop and look. And it'll only take 'em about ten seconds to see sign of me if'n they put nose to ground."

Heck shook his head. "I'm gonna bury your parents, Seeker. It's well past due. They deserve their rest."

"But the Injuns..."

"You don't have to worry about them anymore. Those Injuns come around here again, I'll bury them, too."

Seeker squinted at him, seeming to weigh his words.

Heck stood.

The boy's head tilted, his gaze scaling Heck's long form. "You're the tallest man I ever seen."

Heck nodded. "I've heard that before."

Seeker looked at the bones of his parents then at the broken ground and the tracks he and Heck had made. "You planning on sticking around here, Heck?"

"For a while if you'll have me."

"How long's a while?"

"Depends how long it takes me to find the people I'm hunting. Could be any day now or it might be weeks."

The boy frowned at that. "We can't bury my folks. We gotta cover up these tracks. If you ain't gonna be here—"

"Come with me when I leave."

"And go where?"

Heck shrugged. "Been living in the mountains the last two years, trapping and hunting and fighting Indians. I like to keep moving, see places. Now, I'm hoping to throw in with these folks I mentioned."

"Who are they?"

"A family. They should be passing on the trail before long."

"They kin to you?"

"No. Just good folks. Few years back, they were kind to me when I needed help. See, I'm an orphan, too."

"What's an orphan?"

"Means somebody whose parents have passed on."

"Oh."

"I don't hardly remember my mama, and I wasn't much older than you when Daddy passed over. How old are you, anyway?"

"Eleven, I think. Maybe twelve. Doesn't seem hot enough yet to be my birthday. My birthday's always hot."

"You been alone since the raid?"

Seeker nodded.

"You did good. Staying alive all by yourself, I mean."

"Mostly, staying alive comes down to hiding and covering your tracks." Saying this, the boy's eyes went again to the broken ground and tracks.

Heck could see the kid's mind was chewing on the situation. That was good. That was the sort of thinking that helped you keep your hair in country like this.

But you had to know when you were safe, too, had to learn to breathe easy when the time was right. A perpetually edgy man was nothing more than a squirrel in buckskins.

"Laying low is part of it," Heck agreed, "but there are other ways to stay alive, too. You know how to shoot?"

The boy nodded enthusiastically. "Got me a plains rifle. Ain't dared to fire it since Mama and Daddy got kilt, but I can shoot."

"How come the Indians didn't take the shotgun and the rifle?"

"Daddy was a mountain man. He kept caches here and there in case somebody ransacked the cabin."

"Smart."

"My daddy was the smartest man who ever lived."

"Well, seems like he did a good job raising you."

"Mama was awful smart, too."

"I'll bet. Was she Shoshone?"

Seeker nodded. "She used to sing to me sometimes."

"That must've been real nice."

"It was." The boy's dark eyes were distant for a moment. "I'd like to kill the Injuns who killed them."

"Well, you stick with me, and you might just get the chance. Come on now. Help me dig these graves. It's good and proper."

"Yessir."

When the job was done, Heck could see the boy struggling not to cry, so he told the boy he'd be back and went in and pretended to check on his horses and Burly.

Sometimes, kindness is simple.

When he came back out, the boy's eyes were red and swollen, but he'd dried them.

Heck had the sense not to mention it.

"I got a question for you," Seeker said.

"All right."

"If'n I go with you, wherever you're going to, could we might come back this way someday?"

CHAPTER 21

Hope trudged along as if in a daze, feeling like she was trapped in an endless nightmare.

It could be worse, she reminded herself. *At least Daddy still lives.*

Her father lay in one of the wagons of Basil's father, Mr. Paisley.

Basil had made a big show of it, directing his men to clear a space on the bed of the wagon and disburse the extra supplies across his father's many wagons.

Basil kept flashing smiles at Hope and making grand statements about helping those in need. But she saw no charity in that smile, only triumph and lust.

Daddy had been passing in and out of consciousness for five days since the bandits attacked. He was feverish and had yet to speak.

Dr. Henderson said Daddy's bullet wound was healing well.

He was more concerned with the head injuries Daddy had sustained against the river rocks.

What Daddy really needed, Dr. Henderson explained, was stillness and rest. He was concerned that the constant bumping of the wagon might keep Daddy from healing.

But they could not stop.

That had always been clear, but now it was clearer than ever.

Because the train would not stop. Not for them. Not for anything.

The train rolled on. Always. Or everyone would die.

As would the Mullens if they attempted to stop. First of all, they had no supplies. They had lost everything in the river.

There was no saving their wagon or their poor oxen, who, still hitched to the wagon, had been dragged by the current into a deep hole and drowned.

They might have been able to recover some goods from the river, but they were too concerned with saving Daddy to spare any thought for their possessions, and the train had rolled immediately on, fearing the bandits might return.

Now, the Mullens were utterly destitute and living on the charity of Mr. Paisley.

So far, Basil had been playing the part of the pompous saint, smiling and checking in on them and making a show of every morsel that came their way.

Not that Hope didn't appreciate the kindness. Without it, her family would not survive.

She just wished Basil's motives weren't so obvious.

He'd wanted her the entire trip. And now, he reckoned he had her, reckoned that she owed him whatever he wanted.

He hadn't said so much yet, but she could read the notion in his shining eyes, grating smile, and puffed-out chest.

Sooner or later—and Hope feared it would be sooner—Basil was going to demand payment on whatever bill he was tallying in his mind.

And then what?

He repulsed her. His character was so vile that it soured his wealth and good looks, making them monstrous things.

Even if her heart hadn't belonged to Heck—and it did, of course, and always would—she would have wanted nothing to do with this strutting, mean-spirited young man.

But now, everything had changed.

Her father lay in Basil's wagon, possibly dying, and the Mullens had nothing but their two horses, the clothes on their backs, and Tom's rifle.

They'd lost their wagon, their oxen, their money, their food, their clothing, everything.

Hope didn't even have a dress to wear. She still wore the filthy britches and shirt she'd been wearing when she dove into the river to save her father.

Oh, how miserable she was.

Her cuts and bruises had mostly healed, and she had numbed herself to the constant hunger and fatigue of the trail, but she worried constantly about Daddy and about Basil demanding "payment."

What would she do?

He wanted her as his wife, a fate worse than anything she could imagine.

Almost.

Because on the other side of that particular coin she saw her family abandoned on the trail with no wagon and no supplies, her father wasting away.

Even if they had supplies, they could never walk to Oregon in time to beat the winter.

Besides, the bandits would undoubtedly find them. And even if they evaded the bandits, Indians would scalp them.

So far, the train had experienced no real trouble from Indians. There had been tense moments and tariffs paid for passage across tribal lands, but there had been no raids.

That would be different, Mr. Devereux explained, if there weren't so many wagons in the train.

The Indians targeted smaller trains, generally to steal horses and cattle.

A lone wagon stood next to no chance.

And a few Kentuckians without a wagon would stand no chance at all.

So what would she do, what could she do, when Basil made his demand?

Glancing ahead, she saw Basil riding alongside his father's lead wagon atop his bright white stallion.

Hope shuddered at the sight of him, feeling like an insect trapped in the web of a spider with a pompadour.

And yet, despite her fear and revulsion, she knew what she had to do, no matter how much she hated to do it.

Yes, she would protest and delay and bargain if Basil presented an ultimatum, but eventually, she would have to agree to his demands, no matter the terms.

She would not abandon her family. She would sooner die.

Which was still very much a possibility.

Meanwhile, Hope tossed and turned at night as the big man

and the black man in the pink shirt galloped across her dreams, firing pistols and laughing.

Everyone was tense, awaiting another attack by the bandits. At least two of the bandits had died before they'd ridden off, but seven or eight likely remained.

Mr. Devereux was certain they would return.

"That's the way of men like that," the wagon master explained to the grim survivors around the campfire that night. "They raid like Injuns. They live by the ambush. Hit you hard, see how you take it. You kill a couple of them, they ride off, even if they're winning. But they'll be back. Count on it."

Five men, including both scouts, two women, and a child had died during the attack. Daddy and several others were wounded.

How could they possibly withstand another attack?

Suddenly, absurdly, she wished Heck was here. Somehow, she knew Heck would protect them.

Oh Heck, she thought, *I need you now.*

CHAPTER 22

"Scouts coming," Seeker announced, peering down from the ridge through Heck's spyglass. "Maybe this'll be the Mullens' train."

Heck merely nodded, though his heart set to cantering the way it always did when another wagon train appeared.

Every day, he and Seeker rode up to the trail to check for the Mullens. They traded with the emigrants, who were overjoyed to get potatoes and apples and the fresh meat that Heck and Seeker hunted then strapped onto the backs of the horses.

The boy hadn't lied about being a good shot. He was also a good companion.

They'd been together for the last ten days, and the boy was now like a long-lost little brother to Heck, who'd always wished he'd had a brother.

Seeker was overjoyed to no longer be alone, and he was now excited to ride with Heck, no matter where the trails took them.

They had done a lot of work around the place, cleaning the cabin, tending the garden, and cutting fresh hay.

Through it all, Heck dreamed of Hope, but none of the trains so far had even heard of the Mullens.

Heck knew there was a chance something had happened to them and an even better chance that they'd changed routes at some point and were now hundreds of miles away on another trail like the Santa Fe.

But he didn't think so.

It felt like they were on this trail. And drawing close.

Maybe the two riders down there on the trail were scouting for their train. Maybe he was only an hour or two away from being reunited with the Mullens.

As always, he thought of Hope.

He remembered her beauty, her soft lips, the feel of her against him, and more than anything, her words.

She had confessed her love and said she wanted to marry him.

Had she stayed true to those words to him?

No. It didn't seem possible. How could a girl as lovely and pure as Hope fend off the many suitors sure to be courting her?

So as soon as he thrilled with the possibility of seeing her, he forced himself to stop that line of thinking.

Or tried to, anyway.

And usually failed. Because when he had spoken those same words, he had meant them, and he had stayed true to his vows, despite the lovely, dark-haired girls who'd smiled at him during fandangos in Taos and Santa Fe and the proud young women offered to him as squaws by different tribes.

Most men would have lost their hair, refusing those

arrangements, but Heck had handled the situations diplomatically, expressing his regret and explaining that his religion allowed for only one wife, and he had sworn to marry another.

Besides this diplomacy, his reputation also worked in his favor during those tense moments; for the name of Killing Oak was spoken with reverence among the tribes of the Rockies and plains.

So Heck had kept his vows and preserved himself for Hope in case, against all odds, she had also still clung to the promises they had exchanged on that sun-dappled lane three years earlier.

Now, seeing these scouts, his heart hammered again within his chest, and his skull once more filled with the vision of Hope's loveliness.

And yet he felt something else, too, watching these men.

Caution.

He wasn't sure why. They looked shabby, but so had the other outriders he'd seen.

The other outriders, however, hadn't ridden side by side. They'd spread out and often by some distance.

The pair down below rode slowly at the center of the trail, talking and pointing occasionally at things along the trail.

At one point, the larger of the two—and he was a bull of a man—rode off the trail, dismounted behind a knoll, and laid down on the ground, sighting back toward the trail over an invisible rifle.

His partner, a black man in a pink shirt, followed suit.

What were they doing?

They looked like they were planning an ambush. Maybe

they were being trailed by Indians? Maybe they had led them away from the train and were setting up a surprise.

But Heck's gut said no.

Something felt wrong. Part of it was that shirt.

The scouts he'd seen so far had all ridden brown horses and worn muddy brown, green, or gray clothing that blended with the surrounding country.

So why was this fella wearing a pink shirt?

There was one way to find out.

"I'm gonna go talk to 'em."

"All right," Seeker said. "Let's go."

"Hold on, little brother. I got a funny feeling about these boys. Here's how I want to play it."

Fifteen minutes later, as the men were heading eastward back along the trail, Heck cut in from an angle and called to them from atop a ridge just above their position. One twitch of his reins, and Red would plunge back down the other side, and they'd be off through the scrub.

"Hello, the trail," Heck called.

The men shot away in opposite directions, drew pistols, and wheeled their horses around.

Heck held his Hawken across his lap but did not bother shouldering the weapon.

There was, after all, nothing unusual about their initial reaction… and at this range, they'd have to be both good and lucky with those pistols to so much as graze him before he put a couple of big ol' slugs straight through their chests.

Seeing Heck, the big one smiled. "Greetings, pilgrim!" he hollered uphill in a booming voice.

The other man said nothing but mirrored the big man's smile.

"You boys scouting for a train?" Heck called down.

"What's that?" the big man said, cupping a hand by one ear. "Me and him is a little hard o' hearin'. Might be you could put away that rifle and ride down here and talk?"

Saying this, the men holstered their pistols, so Heck slid the Hawken back in its scabbard and started downhill.

He reined up twenty feet from the men. Up close, they looked mean as rattlers. "You scouting for a train?"

The black man chuckled.

"Yeah, that's it," the big man said. He had a head like a pumpkin and shoulders to match. "We're scouts. Isn't that right, Obadiah?"

"That's right, Keegan. We're scouts." Then, looking back down the trail, Obadiah nodded. "Yonder comes Jack and Bobby."

Heck flicked his eyes in that direction and saw two riders a hundred yards off.

Four scouts? If a train had four scouts, why would they all be riding the same strip of ground? Why wouldn't they be ranging off the trail, hunting game, water, grass, and trouble?

Heck was careful not to let his doubts show. "You wouldn't happen to have a family by the name of Mullen riding along with your train, would you?"

"Mullen?" Keegan said, scratching his big jaw. "That name familiar to you, Obidiah?"

"Nope."

"Sorry, pilgrim. Don't know any Mullens. Where'd you come from? You scouting for a train?"

Heck shook his head. “I'm a mountain man. I live here.”

“By yourself?” Keegan asked.

“All by my lonesome.”

Obadiah chuckled again. He still had one hand on his pistol.

That was okay. So did Heck.

“All right, boys,” he said with a nod. “Happy trails to you.”

“Hold on,” Keegan said. “That's a mighty fine-looking deer you got strapped on the back of your horse.”

“He's for sale. Got some potatoes and apples, too.”

“Trouble is, we ain't got no money,” Keegan said.

Heck reached back with his left hand, loosed the rope, and let the fresh meat fall to the ground. “Here, then. Consider it a gift. I got more than enough, and you boys look like you've been living hard. The deer's yours, free of charge.”

Obadiah chuckled, and Keegan showed Heck his teeth again.

“Well, that's mighty nice of you, pilgrim,” Keegan said. “Now, we'll have the rest of it, too.”

“The rest of it?” Heck said.

“That's right,” Obadiah said, drawing his pistol. “All of it.”

Keegan drew his pistol, too. “I sure like the looks of that horse, mister. I'll ride easier on a nice, big horse like that'n.”

“You should've just taken the meat,” Heck said, raising his hands overhead, appeasing the bandits and giving the signal that Seeker, hidden uphill, had been waiting for.

The Hawken boomed, and Keegan flew out of his saddle.

The bandits' horses shied.

Obadiah cursed and brought up his weapon as Heck drew his Walker Colt.

The bandit fired first. The bullet tugged Heck's shirt but miraculously missed his body.

Heck's bullet plugged Obadiah in the midsection, ruining his pink shirt and knocking him clean out from under his floppy hat.

The bandit dropped his pistol and sagged forward, groaning, as his horse trotted away.

Heck moved, keeping Red close to Obadiah and his horse, using them as a shield against the other bandits, who came charging in, firing their pistols.

One bullet zoomed past Heck's head, passing so close he could hear it split the air.

Another miracle.

Not that he paused to ponder God's grace at that moment.

He was too busy returning fire.

He nailed one of the outlaws in the face—a lucky shot, as he'd been aiming for the chest—pulled back the hammer, and swung his barrel toward the other man, who broke and ran for it.

Uphill, the Hawken boomed again.

The fleeing highwayman flew from his saddle and crunched into the trail without so much as a grunt.

Heck turned back toward Obadiah, but the badman was done for. Growling curses, he dropped from the saddle, one foot still tangled in the stirrup.

The spooked horse charged off, bouncing the bandit's head off the trail.

Obadiah didn't complain. He, like the other bandits, was stone-cold dead.

Seeker came down. The boy was wide-eyed but holding it together, considering he'd just put down two men.

Together, Heck and Seeker gathered the bandits' horses and fallen firearms and searched the dead men.

The loot proved they'd been hitting wagon trains.

As Heck pulled a fistful of fancy jewelry from the big man's pocket, Seeker came over carrying a small leather case. "Look at this, Heck. I never seen anything like it."

Heck took the case and opened it, and all the air rushed from his lungs. His mind reeled with bewilderment.

The glass was cracked, and the silver was tarnished, but Heck would recognize that face anywhere. Over the last three years, a day hadn't passed without him remembering its cherished features.

The daguerreotype depicted Hope Mullen.

The question was, Heck realized, his bones frosting over with dread, where had these bandits gotten it?

CHAPTER 23

The next morning, Basil Paisley rode on the buckboard beside Pearson for an hour before the intolerable Mrs. Mullen finally left her husband's side and exited the wagon.

Without a word to his hired man, Basil slipped back into the wagon and smiled down at the delirious Mr. Mullen.

The man's feverish eyes bulged, and he muttered with agitation but said nothing comprehensible.

Basil crouched beside the fallen man and smiled with triumph. He still remembered the day Mullen had threatened him. Basil was not used to opposition, let alone open threats, so the memory smarted.

Since then, he'd been savoring his bitterness, which now made this moment all the sweeter.

"Not so tough now, are you, Mullen?" Basil chuckled.

Mullen muttered nonsensically, stirring beneath his blankets.

"You sure thought you were tough before, though, didn't

you? You disrespected me. In front of Hope, no less. So now, my dear Mr. Mullen, you are going to pay. Nobody crosses Basil Paisley and gets away with it."

Basil straddled the incapacitated man, using his knees to pin Mullen's arms in place, then reached down and muffled the muttering with his palm. With his other hand, he pinched Mullen's nose shut.

Mullen's eyes bulged. The eyes were far from lucid, but his body apparently understood what was happening, because it thrashed weakly, trying to escape.

But Basil was big and strong and determined, so it was no trouble at all to hold the small man down and smother him.

"So weak," Basil sneered. "Completely in my power. Just like your family is completely in my power. How does that make you feel?"

Mullen struggled, eyes huge and filled with fear.

"Boss," Pearson said, "the womenfolk is coming back."

Basil released Mullen.

The delirious Mullen gasped for air but said nothing, his brain still addled from fever and injury.

"Next time, I'll finish the job," Basil promised the semi-conscious man, "and then I'll have my way with Hope. And if she rejects me, I'll take what I want."

"GOOD MORNING, BASIL," HOPE SAID AS THEY APPROACHED THE wagon, keeping her tone friendly but careful not to sound *too* friendly.

The last thing she needed now was for Basil to read encouragement into her politeness. She had to gently discourage his attentions without offending him.

If she had to surrender to him to save her family, she would. But oh, how she hoped it wouldn't come to that.

"Good morning, Hope," Basil said and gave her a little bow. "I'm hoping to have a word with you… in private."

"Certainly," Hope said, doing her best to remain calm despite the fountain of fear now gushing up inside of her. Was he going to make his demands?

"Excellent," he said. "If you'll excuse us, Mrs. Mullen, Hope and I will just walk on ahead."

"Actually," Hope said quickly, before her mother could respond, "if you don't mind terribly, Basil, Mother and I are in the middle of a very important discussion. Would you mind if we spoke just a little later? I'll come find you."

"Of course." Basil almost covered up his irritation, but his smile didn't quite reach his eyes, which glittered with annoyance.

If he was this entitled now, she thought, what a monstrous husband he would make.

Hope repressed a shudder. "Thank you. I'll see you in a little while."

Basil turned on his heel and marched off, his big shoulders swinging like he was heading into a fight.

Watching him storm off, Hope realized she really did have to talk to her mother. When she had blurted her lie, she'd just been trying to buy time, but she could hold onto her fears no longer. She needed Mother's counsel.

She followed her mother into the wagon to check on Daddy.

Seeing him, fear pierced her heart. "Daddy?"

He had taken a turn for the worse. He moved fitfully, eyes wild with agitation, skin sparkling with perspiration.

Mrs. Mullen mopped his brow. "What is it, Tom?"

His eyes sought her—a good sign, Hope reckoned—but then bulged with desperation.

Hope's heart hammered in her chest. What was wrong? Was Daddy dying?

No, she assured herself, remembering that the doctor said he might get worse before he recovered, that he might fight the stupor as he regained consciousness.

More than anything, he looked desperate to tell them something.

Hope slipped her fingers into his clammy hand. "It's okay, Daddy. We're here with you, and we love you, and you're going to be okay."

His eyes swiveled in her direction and, even though she wouldn't have thought it possible, bulged even more dramatically.

He opened his mouth, trying to speak, but only managed to growl nonsense, the veins in his neck standing out with the effort.

Then he fell back into his bedding, unconscious again.

Once her fright ebbed, Hope was happy to see Daddy resting peacefully. They sat with him for half an hour.

She wanted to talk to her mother about Basil but wouldn't do it here, not with Basil's man driving the wagon and very much within earshot.

Finally, when they were certain the danger was past, Mother said, "Hope, you'd best go and find Basil. A promise is a promise."

"Yes, Mother. But I was wondering if you might walk with me for a moment first? I need your advice."

"Certainly."

They climbed out of the wagon and walked together.

Hope jumped right into it, wanting to talk with Mother before Willa or someone else joined them.

"Basil likes me."

"I know that. But you still don't like him?"

Hope shook her head. "I loathe him."

Her mother frowned.

Hope had expected Mother to counter with Basil's good points—his wealth, his handsome face, his present charity—but she didn't, merely looking thoughtful instead.

Emboldened, Hope spoke the truth. "I still love Heck, Mother. He's the only man I'll ever love."

Mother took her hand, looking sad. "Heck was quite a boy, but my dear, you don't even know if he's still alive."

"I do, though. I know he's alive. I can feel it."

"I hope you're right. I truly do. He's a very nice boy. But Hope, where is he? What's he doing? We have no idea. I'm not trying to be hurtful, but you can't waste your life waiting for a boy you might never see again. Now, Basil—"

"Don't say it, Mother. Don't say I should be with Basil. I can't—"

"I wasn't going to say that, Hope. I was going to say that he is here and has many advantages, as far as potential husbands go. His wealth is obviously part of that. Young women frequently underestimate the importance of money. Many a girl marries for love and lives a life of miserable poverty."

"I'd sooner marry Heck and live in poverty than—"

"Please, child. Let me finish. I was going to say that while Basil has these things going for him, I understand your reservations. I find his self-importance off-putting, and I also suspect that, despite his smiles and polite words, he had a mean spirit. I don't trust him."

"Neither do I, Mother. I don't trust him at all. He terrifies me."

"And you suspect he's going to propose?"

Hope nodded. It felt good to have finally shared her fear.

"Tell him no."

"I'm afraid that if I say no, he'll withdraw his charity."

Mother looked surprised. "Certainly, he wouldn't go as far as..." But she trailed off.

"I'll do it, Mother," Hope said, her eyes filling with tears. "I'll marry him."

Mother's eyes flashed with anger. "Hope Marie Mullen, you will do no such thing!"

"But what if Basil threatens to—"

"I don't care what he threatens," Mother said, and suddenly, she was thrumming with her trademark strength, the exact strength, Hope now realized, that she'd been craving. "We must not fear, Hope. Not even if Basil removes all charity, and we're on our own."

"But Daddy—"

"We must not worry, my child. When you worry, you are not putting your faith in our Lord and savior, Jesus Christ, who told us, *Consider the ravens, for they neither sow nor reap, which have neither storehouse nor barn; and God feeds them. Of how much more value are you than the birds?*"

Hope nodded and bowed her head. She knew Mother was

right, but anxiety nonetheless boiled up within her again. "But what if—"

"Hope, more mistakes have been tendered on 'what if' than any other two words in our language. Have faith. Yes, bad things might come our way. Perhaps even the worst things imaginable.

"But no matter what comes our way, we must hold fast to Jesus through all of it. We must remember that we are not alone. We must stay strong, have faith, and remember that God has a plan.

"A foolish girl might ignore the truth and marry for love, but a girl would be far more foolish to attempt to subvert the will of God. And no matter what lies ahead, I am confident that God would not want you to marry a monster, no matter the threat or consequences."

Hope nodded. She was crying now. It was embarrassing to her, but she couldn't help it.

"My dear child. Don't try too hard. Seek the will of God, and do your best to walk in his light, and regardless of the circumstances, you will know the peace that surpasses all understanding."

CHAPTER 24

Earlier that morning, Heck woke, as was his custom, before first light.

A second later, across the room, Seeker opened his eyes.

The boy was like Heck in that way. Not a light sleeper, necessarily—they both slept like the dead when slumber was upon them—but able to wake into full awareness.

Nearby stood Burly and the horses. Red had wasted no time the night before, putting the four new horses in line. The big stallion's confidence and posture had dominated the geldings instantly. They hadn't so much as whinnied when he'd claimed the buckskin mare.

Burly had simply stood there, watching, looking both bored and amused, a trick all mules are born with.

Heck and Seeker had slept in the stable in case other bandits who'd been riding with those they'd killed might happen upon the bloodshed and follow their tracks back to this place.

Partly, they'd slept in the stable to protect the horses. Partly, they'd slept here because bandits would likely hit the cabin first. And partly, they'd slept here because Burly was good for more than just comical expressions and carrying a heavy load. That mule was a better guard than most watchdogs.

But as it turned out, no one followed them.

And no surprise there. Bandits are cowards by nature. If there were other men, they likely rode up on their dead friends then hightailed it out of the country.

Heck let the horses into the corral and looked around, just to be sure, while Seeker set to making breakfast.

He fed the horses and pulled the daguerreotype once more from his pocket.

Hope's beautiful face stared back at him, filling Heck with concern.

How had these outlaws gotten this? he wondered again, and he could come up with no good way. His best hope was the daguerreotype had fallen along the trail, and these men had found it.

But he doubted that.

At the same time, he had a feeling that Hope was okay. In trouble, maybe, but still alive.

And what's more, he felt certain that she was close.

He raised the daguerreotype to his lips and kissed Hope's image. "I'm coming for you, Hope."

He tucked the picture in his pocket and went into the cabin, where Seeker had pork and beans and coffee ready.

"No tortillas this morning?" Heck asked.

"Figured you'd want to get an early start."

"You figured right, little brother. Let's show this grub who's boss and get gone."

A short time later, they saddled up and headed north. Heck rode Red. Seeker had taken a liking to one of the bandits' horses, a leggy bay he called Boots, on account of the gelding's white stockings.

Heck didn't know horses well enough to judge the overall quality of Boots, but he knew one thing that made Seeker's choice a good one: the bay had barely blinked during the bloodshed. That was a horse a man could count on when the lead flew.

They reached the trail and went first to the scene of the previous night's gunfight.

As Heck had suspected, he saw the tracks of three other horses, all of them shod. The riders hadn't lingered. They'd done a wide circle around the bodies then galloped off, heading the way they'd come.

"Men like that," Heck said, "men who visit trouble upon the undeserving, spend their whole lives looking over one shoulder, waiting for their own turn to roll around."

Heck would be more than happy to give them that turn, but he suspected they had cleared out for greener pastures.

He and Seeker spread out and rode back and forth across the trail, cutting for sign.

No train had passed since the gunfight, so Heck headed east.

When the trail widened, they rode to the north, just in case he'd misjudged the bandits and they might be lying in wait for emigrants.

Later, when Heck saw a solitary rider to the south, he gestured to Seeker and got behind an outcropping topped with swaying grasses. He dismounted, ground hitched Red, crawled to the top of the bluff, and glassed the rider.

The man didn't look like a bandit. Nor did he look like a scout, for that matter.

With his gray hair, plaid waistcoat, and worried expression, he looked like a trail-weary businessman riding alone into the West.

The man rode slowly, almost reluctantly, turning his bespectacled face from side to side, obviously on the watch for trouble.

So, a scout. Even if not much of one.

Perhaps he was a substitute. Perhaps the real scout had been hurt or killed, and this fellow was taking his turn riding at the front of the train.

"What do you reckon, Heck?" Seeker said, having slipped silently up to his elbow.

Heck told him.

"Think a train's comin' soon?"

"I do."

"We gonna ride up on it?"

"I'm pretty comfortable right here, little brother. Lot more comfortable than I'd be if a jumpy new scout started pitching lead in my direction."

"Yeah," Seeker chuckled.

"Let's just sit tight and see what we can see."

"All right."

They didn't have to wait long. A wagon appeared, followed by another, then others.

Like the lone rider, the drivers of these wagons were scanning the surrounding country warily.

So they'd had trouble. Likely with the bandits he'd killed.

"You see her?" Seeker asked, his voice edged with excitement.

Heck wasn't much for confessing his dreams and feelings, but he'd spent every hour of every day with Seeker, and he liked the boy, and as they'd weeded the vegetable patch, cleaned the cabin, and planted summer crops like tomatoes, squash, and peppers, Heck had told him a bit about Hope, leaving out the kissing but confessing that he had tender feelings for her and hoped she still felt the same way toward him.

"No, I—" Heck started, and then his words died as his heart shook and bounced like the heavy bag back in Paddy Corcoran's gym.

It was Hope.

CHAPTER 25

She was taller, her face was drawn and dirty, and her auburn hair no longer shone so brightly, but he would recognize her anywhere, and nothing had ever looked half so lovely to his eyes.

"It's her," he said, nearly groaning the words. "It's Hope."

Suddenly, this towering, powerful mountain man, who was feared all up and down the Rockies and normally carried himself with all the stony stoicism of the Spartan warriors he'd read about in the officers' books back at Fort Bent, was swimming in a sea of emotion.

He was so happy to see Hope his heart was fit to burst. She was alive, and she was here!

But at the same time, he suddenly felt more dread than he would if a grizzly were charging him.

Because seeing her, knowing that he was about to ride down there and say hello, he felt something he hadn't felt in years: self-conscious.

All at once, he realized how dirty and bedraggled he was in his filthy buckskins and his unwashed beard. A painful memory returned to him then, the memory of how he'd reacted to Rabbit Foot's stench the first time they'd met on the porch of Plank's Trading Post.

He shook his head with dismay.

Did Heck stink like that now?

He must. After all, he'd lived alongside the old mountain man for years, doing what he did, eating what he ate, forgoing baths and soaking his duds in every manner of blood and dirt and grime.

Why hadn't he thought of this before? Why hadn't he bathed and put on his clean shirt?

Seeing Hope down there, he felt nearly insurmountable shame.

How could he ride down there and let her see and smell him like this?

"Ready, big brother?" Seeker asked, plainly excited.

"Not quite, Seeker. I gotta think things through for a second."

"Think things through? That's her, ain't it?"

"It's her, all right. That's the problem. I just realized what I must look like. And smell like."

"Oh."

"Yeah, oh. I'm thinking maybe I ought to ride back to your place and jump in the creek and change my shirt at least."

"Might not be a bad idea, Heck. You do smell riper'n a green pelt."

Heck nodded, knowing it was the truth. But he couldn't

quite bring himself to stand and mount up, couldn't bring himself to even give Seeker a turn with the spyglass.

He couldn't stop staring at Hope.

Seeing her lovely face, he felt all warm inside. But the longer he watched her, the more he realized something was wrong.

Hope didn't look happy. And it wasn't just trail weariness.

She looked sad. And maybe frightened.

Why?

Whatever the case, he realized he couldn't wait a second longer. Yes, he stunk to high Heaven, but he couldn't bear to spend one more moment away from Hope.

"I've changed my mind," Heck said. "Come on, little brother."

They mounted up and came around the bluff without hurrying because they knew if they went thundering down there, someone was liable to mistake them for bandits and open fire.

For the same reason, he approached the front of the column, not the middle, where Hope was walking. He would clear the guards, state his business, dismount, and surprise her on foot. He wanted to be right up on her when she recognized him.

He grinned, more excited than he'd ever been in his life. How long he had dreamed of this moment!

When a man spotted them and shouted to the others, Heck put on a smile and raised his hands.

After a brief discussion and much searching of the horizon, three men saddled up and approached Heck and Seeker, rifles at the ready.

Two of them looked frightened. The third, a grizzled man with hard eyes, looked merely wary.

He was the one who did the talking when the trio reined in thirty feet away. "What's your business?"

Heck nodded. "Name's Heck Martin, and before you ask, Heck's short for Hector. I'm awful glad to see you."

"Why's that?" the man said.

"I set out from Bent's Fort several weeks ago to find this wagon train. I believe my dear friends, the Mullens, are traveling with you. I come to help them get where they're going."

The men relaxed at the mention of the Mullens' name.

The grizzled man rode forward and stuck out his hand. "Good to meet you, Heck. My name's Cap Devereux. I'm the wagon master. I apologize for the cold welcome, but we've had trouble with bandits recently."

Heck smiled at that. "Well, I don't think you'll be having any more trouble with them. Me and Seeker killed four of them, and I believe the others turned tail and ran."

"Killed them? When?"

"Last night. I been watching the trail up ahead. Saw them coming, gave them some fresh game, apples, and potatoes, and they tried to pay me in lead. Lucky for me, my little brother here was uphill with his Hawken."

"Well, that certainly is good news," Devereux said. "They gave us a lot of trouble. I'm afraid they gave the Mullens trouble, too."

Heck stiffened. "What do you mean?"

"The bandits hit us at a river crossing. Mr. Mullen was shot."

Just like that, Heck was filled with horror. Though he'd only stayed with the Mullens for a short while, that time had never quit resonating in his memory or his soul. Mr. Mullen had been like a second father to him, especially during those early, hard months in St. Louis. "He's not dead?"

"No, but he's in bad shape. Doc doesn't know if he'll make it or not."

"Where is he?"

Devereux hooked a thumb. "Back a ways. He's riding in one of Paisley's wagons. The Mullens lost their wagon in the attack, lost everything."

"But the others—Mrs. Mullen, Hope, Tom—they're okay?"

Devereux nodded. "Unharmed but struggling, as you might imagine."

"I gotta see them."

"All right, Heck. You're welcome here. Hope you and... Seeker, is it? Hope you boys'll be sticking with us. Seems like you know how to handle yourselves, and we could use the help. I lost two scouts in the attack, and the other's laid up with a gunshot wound that's smelling worse every day."

Heck nodded. "We'll give you a hand. Now, if you'll excuse me..."

"Go ahead, son. Go see your people."

"Hey," one of the other men hollered as Heck and Seeker rode off. "You got any more of them apples?'

As they drew closer to where he'd seen Hope walking, Heck stopped Red and dismounted and handed the reins to Seeker, explaining, "I want to walk up on her."

Seeker grinned. "You want me to stay here, Heck?"

"Nah. Just give me a minute then come on along behind me. I can't wait for Hope to meet my little brother."

The boy beamed at that. "Good luck, Heck."

"Thanks, Seeker." He felt another wave of self-consciousness. "Looking like I do and smelling like I do, I need all the luck I can get."

Despite these concerns, he strode forward. It took all his self-discipline to keep from grinning like a fool.

He was concerned for Mr. Mullen—deeply concerned—and sorry to hear the Mullens had lost everything, but he had already mentally committed himself to doing whatever he could to help them, so he dismissed those concerns now and focused solely on the moment at hand: his long-awaited, long-dreamed-of reunion with Hope.

And there she was!

He stuck to the north of her, traveling among the wagons, hoping to get right up on her before he gave a casual hello. That would really tickle her.

As he watched, however, Hope caught up to a man riding on a fancy-looking horse. Fancy-looking for sure, but only a fool would ride a white horse in this country. Indians would see you from miles away.

Hope hailed the man.

He stopped his horse and hopped gracefully down and waited for her.

Hope smiled.

The man was young and big and muscular, all decked out in clothes that were just as fancy as that white horse of his and just about as sensible. Those duds wouldn't last five minutes off the trail.

But he was all duded up and had glossy mutton chops and a whole bunch of black hair piled up on top of his head. It waggled when he bowed to Hope.

Oh no, Heck thought, as the pair came together and the big young dandy took her hand and kissed the knuckles. *I'm too late. She's hitched her wagon to this character.*

He couldn't walk over to Hope now, looking and smelling like he did, especially if she'd thrown in with that big dandy.

Disappointment lanced his heart, slicing it in half.

Maybe he'd better just ride off forever.

CHAPTER 26

Hope held her polite smile. It wasn't easy. The touch of Basil's lips against the back of her hand sickened her to her core.

"You wanted to talk to me?" she asked, trying to keep her tone one shade warmer than neutral.

"Yes," Basil said, still holding onto her hand.

She forced herself not to pull away.

He drew himself up and lifted his chin slightly, smiling down with that smug satisfaction mastered only by the wealthy. "The time has come, Hope, for you to choose. Say you will be mine, and I'll have the minister marry us tonight when we stop to make camp. You'll move into my wagon, and I will make sure your family has everything they need from here to Oregon and after we arrive." His smile broadened with pride. "It's a very generous offer."

Hope nodded. "It's very generous indeed, Basil. Thank you, and if my situation were different, I would happily accept, but

I've been in love with the same man since I was fourteen years old."

Basil dropped her hand, and his eyes flashed with impatience. "Your situation, in case you haven't noticed, is one of utter destitution. Without my help, you and your precious family would be dead in a matter of days."

Now, Hope thought, *now is the time to tread carefully.*

She had given it to him straight, had told him the truth, and it felt wonderful, reminding her of what Mother always said: *the truth will set you free.*

But now Hope had to stay strong and help Basil to save face because he was very proud and not used to being denied anything. And what he had said about their chances without his help was completely true.

So she spoke with a soft voice and a submissive expression. "And we are so grateful to you and your father, Basil. So very grateful. We know that you rescued us and know that we live only because of your—"

"If you reject me, it's over," he snapped, his face going a deep purple. "I'm cutting off all help immediately."

Hope pretended shock. "You wouldn't. Basil, please, I beg you—"

"Save it, girl. The time for batting lashes is over. Accept my offer and save your family or reject me and suffer the consequences."

"Please, Basil, we need your help. Your kindness is so—"

"No more prattling," Basil snapped. "Yes or no, girl?"

Hope was a pillar of flame, burning with anger and fear and more than anything else, resolve.

She blinked up at this haughty monster, knowing she could

never marry him, and said a silent prayer. There was nothing she, herself, could do in this moment to save her family. She could only embody her name and hope against all hope that God would soften Basil's heart.

"If you will not hear my pleas," she said, staring into his raging eyes, "if you must have a simple yes or no at this moment, then you already have my answer. No."

Basil balled his big hands into fists. His face shifted from red to purple.

For a second, Hope thought he was going to strike her, but she stood her ground.

Basil turned to his two men, who stood a short distance off. "Go kick the Mullens out of my wagon!"

"Basil, please, don't. Not Daddy. If you kick him out now, he'll die."

"Then let him die! You had your chance, girl. You men, get him out!"

"Where you want us to put him, boss?"

"Put him on the ground," Basil said with a nasty smile. "He'll be in it soon enough thanks to her stubbornness."

The two men grunted and walked off.

Hope watched them go with a stab of terror. "Basil, please have mercy."

"No. There will be no mercy for you. Not even if you relent. You had your chance, and you wasted it. No one disrespects Basil Paisley and gets away with it."

"But what will we do?"

"You'll beg for help, that's what you'll do. And by the end of this trip, you'll all die. But first, you'll become a worn-out, two-bit prostitute."

She stared at him, shocked by his cruelty and venom.

"Out here in the wilderness, I am God," Basil sneered. "I giveth and I taketh away. And I'm going to take everything from you." He reached out and snatched up her wrist in an iron grip.

"Let me go, please."

He pulled her closer. "No."

"Please stop. You're hurting me."

"Get used to it. I can do anything I want to you. Maybe I'll throw you down and take you right here, right now, where everyone can hear you scream. Who will even dare to try to stop me? Your daddy? No, he's a dead man. Your brother? He's no bigger than you. Who will protect you now?"

CHAPTER 27

"I will protect her now and forevermore," Heck growled, stepping forward, ready to kill. He'd been ready to leave, figuring Hope loved this man. Then, he'd heard her tone, approached from an angle, and heard the end of their exchange. Now, his voice was solemn steel, every word an eternal vow. "Take your hand off her or lose the fingers."

The guy with the hair—Hope had called him Basil—yanked his hand back like he'd touched a burning log. His eyes reeled with terror but rapidly shifted, darkening with white-hot rage at having been humiliated.

Basil raised his hand halfway as if to again grab hold of the lovely girl. Hope stared wide-eyed not at Basil but at a face Heck now realized she might not even recognize due to the passage of three years, the filth, and the full black beard.

But even as these thoughts occurred to Heck, even as her tormentor, Basil, stood there in an agony of inaction, torn between cruelty and cowardice, Hope cried out, "Heck! I knew you would save me! I prayed to God, and He has rewarded my faith!"

She rushed to Heck and threw her arms around him and hugged him fiercely, sobbing with joy.

Heck flattened one big hand on her small back and pinned her to him, loving the feel, at long last, of Hope against him.

Basil flexed his big muscles and looked Heck up and down with a condescending smile. "You were saving yourself for this yokel? Hope, I never dreamed you were so—"

"Mind your tongue, boy," Heck interrupted. "You speak unkindly of Hope again, your teeth will wish you hadn't."

"Boy?" Basil shrieked. "Do you have any idea who I am? I am Basil Rutherford Paisley!"

"Good for you," Heck said. "Hope, it sure is nice to see you again after all this time."

Hope leaned back and smiled up at him, her bright green eyes glistening with tears. "Oh, Heck, it's so good, a dream come true. We've had an awful hard time of it."

"Well, I'm here now. I'll take care of you."

"Take care of her?" Basil laughed nastily. "With what? You don't even have a wagon." His eyes flicked to where Seeker was riding up, trailing Red. "Perfect! And this filthy little savage is with you?"

"I told you to mind your tongue," Heck said, releasing Hope and stepping toward Basil. "That kid's only eleven, but he's already ten times the man you'll ever be. Now, take it back and apologize."

Basil laughed haughtily. "I never apologize."

Heck shrugged and started forward. "Well, you're gonna wish you had."

Basil hopped away with an amused smile and raised his big fists in a practiced boxing stance. “Be warned, sir. I am a trained fighter. Father bought me lessons with the New York State boxing champion, Del Brucker!”

Heck didn’t even bother raising his hands. He hadn’t boxed for three years, but after growing up in the mountains of Kentucky and spending hundreds of rounds in the ring, fighting was as natural to him as blinking his eyes.

Basil tensed, eyes bulging, telegraphing his attack and making it easy for Heck to evade a spirited three-punch combination.

Heck clipped Basil with a jab. Then, knowing Basil would come straight back at him, he cocked his shoulder and nailed him with a right hand that broke Basil’s aristocratic nose and sat him down hard on his backside.

Up on the bay gelding, Seeker laughed like he’d never seen anything so funny.

Outraged, a bloodied Basil struggled to his feet and leveled a finger at the boy. “Shut up, you filthy breed!”

“See,” Heck said calmly, “that’s the sort of talk that got you into trouble in the first place.”

He stepped forward, batted away Basil’s desperate haymaker, and unloaded with both hands, rocking the cruel bigmouth with half a dozen hooks and crosses that left Basil stretched on the ground, clutching his ruined face and crying with a pitiful lack of self-respect that turned Heck’s stomach.

Heck loomed over him. He wasn’t even winded. “You want more or have you had enough?”

Basil waved him off. “Had… enough.”

“Apologize.”

"Sorry, kid."

Seeker threw back his head and laughed louder.

"Now to Hope."

Basil swung his hateful gaze from Heck to Hope. "Sorry, Hope."

Heck nodded. "All right, then. I guess we're through. Oh, and Del Brucker wasn't a bad fighter, as long as he had the upper hand. But he lacked heart, like you. When I was fifteen, I broke his ribs in the 27th round, and he laid down and curled up like a little baby."

CHAPTER 28

"Look out, Heck," Hope said. "Basil's men are coming."

Heck turned and saw two rough-looking characters running over.

They stopped ten feet away and stood with their hands on their pistol grips, ready to draw.

Heck dropped his hand to his Colt. "Hope, get on back behind the horses."

"Yes, Heck," she said retreating behind Red.

Seeker had his Hawken trained on Basil's men.

And there, behind the two thugs, was none other than Hope's brother, Tom, hurrying this way with a rifle.

Heck said, "You boys draw those guns, you're dead."

Basil, who'd been sitting there feeling sorry for himself, spotted his men and laughed with triumph. "He can't beat both of you. Shoot him!"

But the men hesitated, flexing their hands and looking frightened.

"I don't need to beat both of 'em," Heck said. "You boys ever see the size of a hole a plains rifle makes in a man?" He nodded toward Seeker, who panned his muzzle back and forth from one thug to the other.

"My rifle makes a pretty good mess, too," Tom said from behind the outgunned men, who lifted their hands in the air, knowing they were beat.

"Shoot him, you cowards!" Basil demanded, pulling himself off the ground. "Shoot him!"

"That's enough of that kind of talk," Mr. Devereux said, coming over with a crowd of others, most of them armed. "Everybody put your guns down."

Seeker and Tom both looked to Heck.

He nodded, and they lowered their barrels.

"Now what in tarnation is going on here?" Mr. Devereux demanded.

"This man assaulted me!" Basil shrieked. "He invaded our wagon train and attacked me without provocation!"

Several people who'd witnessed the altercation spoke at once, putting Basil's lies to shame.

Devereux turned to Heck and raised a silver brow. "Well, son, let's hear your side of it."

"I came over to see Hope, and this fella had her by the wrist. Wouldn't let her go. And he was saying the most awful things I ever heard a man say to a woman."

"Lies!" Basil squawked, holding his bleeding nose.

"It's the truth," Hope said. "Every word of it."

Heck nodded at her and continued. "So I told him to let her go and mind his tongue. He sassed me some, but I didn't mind too much until he insulted my brother. I gave him the chance to apologize. He refused.

"So we settled our differences like men. He took the first swing. Trouble is, he can't fight. I stretched him out and gave him another chance to apologize. This time, he was gentle as a lamb, at least until his buddies showed up. He kept telling them to shoot me, but they knew better. Then y'all came over."

"Lies!" Basil shouted. "These two are bandits! They're some of those who attacked us. That's it. I saw them. I saw them back at the river. They were riding with those murderers!"

A tense silence followed. Folks eyed Heck, likely hunting for anything familiar.

"How'd you see the bandits when you were hiding in your daddy's wagon?" Devereux asked with half a smile.

"You don't talk to me like that, Devereux, or I'll make sure you never get another wagon master job!"

Devereux's smile broadened. "Do you promise? After traveling with the likes of you, Basil, I've lost my stomach for the work."

"My father pays you to take care of things. If this is how you handle a crisis, he won't pay you one more penny!" Basil screamed.

Devereux's smile died, and his eyes hardened. "You talk a tough one. If your father won't pay me, I'll pull out… now. Good luck making it the rest of the way without me."

"Well, if you don't need anything else, Mr. Devereux," Heck said, "we'll be going. Sounds like Mr. and Mrs. Mullen need our help."

"You're not going anywhere!" Basil shouted. "You're going to pay for your crimes!"

"Contrary to what this boy seems to think," Devereux said, "I am still the wagon master, and you folks are free to go."

"This isn't over!" Basil screamed, pointing to Heck. "I'm going to get you for this!"

Heck, who had started to leave, turned back and gave Basil a hard look. "That tongue of yours is a troublesome thing. Never talk like that unless you mean it."

"I do mean it. You'll see. I'm going to kill you!"

"Well, then, you had better steer clear of me. I don't take threats lightly. I see you again, I'll assume you're coming for me and put you down like a mad dog."

With that, Heck turned and left.

Basil shouted after him, "You won't even see me coming!"

"Oh, Heck," Hope said, taking his arm. "Thank you so much. I just knew you would show up when I needed you most."

"I'm thankful I was here," Heck said. Then, nodding behind him, he added, "and I'm glad Seeker was here too. Good work with the Hawken, little brother."

Smiling, the boy nodded.

Heck turned to Tom, seized his hand, and pumped it up and down, thanking him for showing up when needed, too. "I outgrew the boots you made me, but if you look on that big, red stallion yonder, you'll see I'm still using the saddle you worked on."

Tom was clearly thunderstruck to see Heck again. "I just can't believe it," he said. "You're really here. Hope always said you'd come back, but it didn't seem possible."

Heck introduced Hope and Tom to Seeker, and Hope thanked the boy for helping out.

Then, smiling up at Heck, Hope said, "You're even taller than you were last time I saw you."

"Three years will do that to a person," Heck said with a grin. "I must say you've changed, too."

For some reason, this made Hope frown. She raised a hand to her long, auburn locks, which had lost much of their luster and lay limply across the shoulders of her dirty shirt. "Oh, Heck, I know I look a sight. How many times I've dreamed of seeing you again, and in exactly zero of those daydreams did I look so horrendous."

"Hope," Heck said, his voice going low, "you look more beautiful than I remember, more beautiful than anything I've ever seen."

Hope blushed and stifled a laugh. "You lie, Heck Martin, but I appreciate it, considering the circumstances. That beard of yours. Doesn't it get itchy?"

"Don't really notice it. Keeps me warm during winter in the mountains, though." Suddenly, he remembered his filthy state and felt self-conscious all over again. It was a strange thing for a young man who'd long ago quit worrying what others thought about him. He touched his beard. "Do you hate it?"

"Hate it? I absolutely love it, Heck. You look so rugged and masculine."

Heck didn't know what to say to that and was surprised to feel his face go hot beneath his beard. Was he blushing? He wouldn't have even thought that possible. But then again, Hope had always had a gift for surprising him.

Up ahead, folks were gathered in a circle, looking down at something on the ground.

Hope gave a little cry, and they rushed forward.

"Please, there has to be some way," Mrs. Mullen pleaded with a short, bespectacled man, who shook his head and offered a sad smile.

On the ground before them, Mr. Mullen lay atop a stretcher, thrashing weakly. Beneath the bloody bandage covering his forehead, his eyes burned with fever or pain or both.

Heck grunted at the sight of him, feeling like he'd been punched in the liver. He'd never met anyone as full of life and optimism and kindness as Mr. Mullen, but now the man looked inches from death.

"I'm so terribly sorry, Mrs. Mullen," the bespectacled man said. "I truly am."

"But Dr. Henderson, my husband needs the medicine."

"The wagon train needs the medicine," the man said firmly but not cruelly. "What if someone else needs it a few miles down the trail? I'm sorry, Mrs. Mullen, but I couldn't possibly give it to you."

"Then sell it to me," Heck said, stepping forward.

"Who are you?" the doctor said.

"Heck?" Mrs. Mullen said, smiling incredulously through her tears. "Heck, is it really you?"

Heck swept the filthy hat from his head and nodded. "Yes, ma'am, it's really me, and I sure am sorry I didn't get here sooner."

"Oh, Heck, I am so happy to see you." She blinked at the sky. "Thank you, Jesus. Thank you, Lord."

"I'm glad you're here to help, young man," the doctor said. "I truly am. These poor people need all the help they can get. They have no wagon and no money, and Mr. Mullen is, as I'm sure you can see, very gravely injured."

"Will he get better?" Heck asked, just wanting to get to the truth.

The doctor spread his small hands. "Who can say? He's very tough, and he has been showing some signs of possible recovery. Also, I think he'll stand a better chance of recovery if he's not jostling up and down in a wagon, but I have to wonder... I mean, the train will keep rolling on, you understand, so if the Mullens are all alone..."

"They're not alone. I'm with them. So is Seeker. And he's got a place not far from here. You don't mind if the Mullens stay with us, do you, little brother?"

The boy shook his head. "I'd like that, Heck."

"It's settled then," Heck said. "Normally, I'd make a travois and drag a wounded man behind old Red, but Tom and me can carry Mr. Mullen. Right, Tom?"

"Right, Heck. We'll carry him."

"It ain't but a short walk. Two, three miles."

Mrs. Mullen hesitated, glancing toward the wagon train and beyond toward, Heck assumed, Oregon and the life she had planned to make there. She had a streak of silver in her hair that hadn't been there three years earlier.

Heck waited, saying nothing, knowing the woman was struggling to come to terms with a huge change of plans.

Then Mrs. Mullen nodded to herself and showed him that wonderful, motherly smile he had missed so much. "Thank you very much, Heck, and thank you, Seeker. We are much obliged to you both, I'm sure."

The last of the wagons were rolling past.

"I am pleased to know that you'll have assistance, Mrs.

Mullen," the doctor said, touching his hat. "I wish you all well, but I should be going now."

"Hold on," Heck said. "What about that medicine?"

The doctor looked uncomfortable. "Perhaps with rest, Mr. Mullen won't need—"

"I'll give you fifty dollars right now," Heck said, reaching into his jacket and pulling out golden coins that winked in the sunlight.

"Fifty dollars?" the doctor said, and Heck, who'd haggled all over the frontier, knew he had him.

Not wanting to delay their departure, however, Heck nailed it down. "All right, doc, you drive a hard bargain. I'll give you a hundred dollars for the medicine and that stretcher."

CHAPTER 29

Hope rode as if in a dream, bobbing gently up and down atop Dolly's back, moving steadily away from the trail. Until this moment, the notion of braving the wilderness had been the stuff of nightmares; beyond were savages, wild animals, starvation, thirst, and death.

And yet now, following Heck, Hope felt the first peace she had known in weeks.

Heck's size was part of it, as was his capability—how easily he had handled Basil—but mostly, it was his confidence; that and the strong sense of God's hand at work, Heck showing up when he did, answering her prayers, saving her and her family in their direst moment of need.

Of course, they were far from safe. It felt reckless, carrying her father off into the unknown; but again, with Heck leading the way, she dismissed worry and had faith.

She rode beside Mother just behind Heck and Tom, who carried Daddy on the stretcher Heck had purchased, along with the medicine, from Doctor Henderson. They moved slowly, keeping the stretcher as steady as possible. Daddy lay still but looked placid. She hoped the doctor was right, hoped that the lack of jarring would help him recover.

Staring at Heck, taking in his great height and powerful frame, his intense eyes and black beard and the ease with which he carried his end of the stretcher, she felt a surge of optimism. Perhaps Daddy would be okay after all.

A glance toward Mother made her feel better still. Mother rode with a slight smile brightening her exhausted features.

It was a stolen glance—Mother didn't know anyone was looking at her—so that slight smile warmed Hope's heart all the more. She had glimpsed a private moment, a *true* moment, her mother smiling despite the challenges behind and before them.

Knowing Mother, she was probably lost in a reverie, praising God for their deliverance.

Which sounded like a great idea to Hope.

For the next few minutes, Hope followed what she believed to be Mother's lead, thanking God reverently and repeatedly for saving them from all manner of destruction.

Once she finished, she felt better than ever, so light and happy, she almost felt like she was floating through the air.

Heck looked so tall and handsome, so strong and masculine. His face and clothes were dirty, and she could smell him from atop Dolly, but none of that bothered her.

He'd been out in the mountains, after all. And besides, she wasn't exactly as fresh as a flower herself these days.

It was so exciting and wonderful to see him grown into such a man. Her heart ached as she studied every angle of his face, staring at her long-savored dream come to life again.

Did he still have feelings for her, though?

Clearly, he cared for her and her family. He'd come all this way to save them, and he'd said that he would protect her.

But men protected friends and sisters, too. They even protected livestock.

So yes, he cared for her, but did he still have romantic feelings for her?

For her part, Hope had never stopped loving Heck, had never stopped dreaming of their reunion.

But what about him?

They had been apart for three years, and he was so handsome. There had to be other girls.

A sudden fear gripped her. Did Heck have a woman? A wife, perhaps, or a squaw? Would she be waiting for them wherever they were headed?

Oh, how hard it would be to receive hospitality from any such woman.

As she stared at Heck's handsome face and powerful shoulders, this fear swelled. Such a handsome, rugged, capable man couldn't possibly be alone, could he? He had to have a woman waiting for him.

Unless he really did love her. Unless Heck, like Hope, had indeed waited all these years, cherishing the short but incredibly sweet time they had spent together back in Kentucky.

It seemed too wonderful a prospect to possibly be true, so she forced her mind away from it and studied the surrounding country.

The path followed a stream through a high-walled canyon. Sage brush and grass crowned the upper rims, while aspen and lodgepole pines covered the slopes. Down in the basin, these conifers gave way to cottonwoods, birch, willows, and a colorful explosion of dandelions, shooting stars, and Indian paintbrush.

Birds and squirrels moved in the trees, and they startled a herd of deer that went bounding off, their white tails bobbing up and down like seesaws as they disappeared into a pocket of darker pines.

This was a lovely place, and Hope thought its beauty would prove downright heartbreaking when the aspens turned yellow.

Noticing the sweat rolling down Tom's neck, Hope dismounted and asked to take a turn at helping Heck to carry Daddy.

"I'm all right," Tom claimed, but she could see he was struggling.

"I know, but I'd like to talk with Heck," she said, wanting to give Tom a chance to save face.

"All right, Hope," Tom said. "Let me know when you get tired."

Tom and Heck set Daddy gently on the ground. Then she and Heck picked him back up again.

How light her father felt. It troubled her. He was not a large man, but he had always been strong, a hard worker without an ounce of quit in him.

At least until the bandits attacked. Even then, even gunshot, he'd been fighting to keep their oxen moving and their wagon upright. But the Cranstons' wagon had slammed into theirs and knocked him into the river, and the rocks and rapids had done the rest.

Would he ever come back to them?

Yes. He was a fighter. He would come back to them.

She couldn't imagine any other reality. And now that Heck was with them, it was easier to believe.

Daddy would survive.

But would he ever be the same? Would he still be the tireless, encouraging, kind-hearted father who loved to make her laugh?

She hoped so. She surely hoped so.

"He'll be all right," Heck said, apparently reading her worries, and then he put voice to her thoughts. "He's a fighter. He knows how to battle back. Everybody gets knocked down sooner or later. What matters is having the heart to stand up again. And your daddy has heart."

"Thanks, Heck," Hope said, feeling a sudden lump in her throat. "It sure is good to see you again."

"It's wonderful to see you, Hope. You look beautiful." An awkward smile split his beard, and he surprised her by blushing.

"Beautiful?" she laughed. "I look like forty miles of rough road. I'm dirty, my hair's a mess, and—"

"And you're still the most beautiful thing I've ever seen. Not just the most beautiful girl. The most beautiful thing. And I've traveled some awful pretty country these last few years. I've seen dew sparkling on high meadows full of lupine. I've looked down from stony peaks and watched sunlight flash off the feathers of eagles soaring below me. I've watched rainbows form in the mist of thundering waterfalls never before seen by any white man. And none of it holds a candle to your present beauty."

Now, it was Hope's turn to blush. "Why, Heck, you're a poet."

"A poet?" he laughed. "Not hardly. I'm just a man setting eyes on the prettiest girl who ever lived."

"Oh Heck, you're just—"

"Don't, Hope," Heck interrupted. "I say what I mean and mean what I say. I want to speak my mind, but if you don't like me talking that way, I'll stop."

He stared at her so intensely, it made her heart hammer, and she had to look away.

When she lifted her eyes again, she forced a smile onto her hot face. "It's okay, Heck. I like to hear you say it. I want you to always tell me what you think and how you feel. Always."

"Likewise, Hope. You can tell me anything."

Happiness surged up in her then, and she felt a wild impulse to blurt out all her feelings and questions. Most of all, she wanted to ask if he still loved her and planned to marry her.

But she held her tongue.

After all, Heck was nothing if not compassionate. He had saved her again, had saved her whole family this time, and if he knew she wanted him to marry her, well, he'd likely propose right this moment.

And for as much as she wanted that to happen, she didn't want to force any profession of love, let alone a marriage proposal, especially not under these conditions.

As they walked, they talked about the last three years. Heck wanted to know all about her life, not just the trials of the trail but also the time before, so she told him about the farm and the days she'd spent there, riding Dolly and helping Mother, and shared little stories, like when Tom made a saddle for the governor's nephew or when a neighbor had spoken rudely to Mother and Daddy had gone over and knocked him out cold or when Mama had won the blue ribbon for her pie in town two summers back.

Heck loved her stories, but when she questioned him, and he talked about living alone in St. Louis and prizefighting and exploring the wilderness and hunting big game and fighting Indians, she felt silly for the stories she'd told. She marveled at how much Heck had seen and done, at how much he'd lived since she'd last seen him. By comparison, she felt like a child tottering away from its mother for the first time.

Then Seeker, who'd been riding in front, descended an embankment and crossed the stream, and they traveled alongside a bench covered in a sight for sore eyes: a bright green stand of knee-high corn.

Her mouth dropped open, all but tasting the kernels it would bear.

Heck smiled at her, and they entered a beautiful clearing populated by a cabin, a corral, a tidy vegetable garden, and an orchard of neatly pruned apple trees. "Welcome home, Hope."

CHAPTER 30

Basil fumed.

"I brought you west to make you a man," his father snapped, "and here you are, throwing a temper tantrum like a little boy. You're lucky you didn't get killed."

Basil stood there, trembling with rage, wanting to lock his big hands around his father's neck and choke the life from him. He was sick of his father's lecture and condescending tone and enraged that his father was talking loudly enough that others could hear his words.

That, more than anything.

Because Basil refused to be mocked. He'd sooner kill someone than hear them laugh at his expense.

But he would not kill his father. Not yet.

Because the man was still of use to him. As the oldest son, Basil would inherit his father's fortune… as long as he made the man's death look like an accident.

But Basil wanted more than that. He wanted the dream he

had latched onto. He wanted to be a big man in the West. The biggest man. He wanted not only his father's present fortune but also whatever fortune his father would build in the West.

And that was why the man was still of use to him, why Basil would not kill him immediately.

Basil hated work. It was tiresome and draining and kept him from things he'd rather do. But his father thrived on hard work and always had. Which boggled Basil's mind. Why work when you had enough money to hire someone else to labor for you?

So the plan stayed the same. Continue to play the mostly obedient son, reach Oregon, and do just enough to stay in Father's good graces while the man built a new empire in the West.

Then, once that empire was firmly established, Father would have an accident.

And Basil would assume his rightful position atop the throne of power. All while barely lifting a finger, showing how much smarter he was than his bullheaded father.

"And the things you were saying to that girl," his father growled, going purple in the face. "Mr. Thompkins is saying you told her—"

"Thompkins is a liar!" Basil shouted, mentally adding Thompkins to the long list of people who would eventually feel his wrath. "He's jealous!"

Basil's father just stared at him for a few silent seconds. Then he shook his head and finally lowered his voice. "Part of the reason I brought you west was the incident."

Basil managed not to roll his eyes. "I know, Father."

"What you did to that girl, Basil. You said it was the alcohol. You said—"

"It was the alcohol, Father. And I told you, she asked me to do those things."

"I find that hard to believe, Basil. I truly do. But then again, the older you get, I find more and more of what you say hard to believe. Whatever the case, your stunt with that girl certainly cost me dearly."

"I'm sorry, Father," Basil said, remembering how exhilarating it had been, tying up that stupid farm girl and hurting her.

Only now, standing here and playing the role of the remorseful son, did he realize some part of him had all along been planning to do the same things to Hope. He grew hot, thinking of it. How he would love to pinken her pale flesh with a switch. How delicious her screams would be.

He was so lost in the fantasy that he nearly missed what his Father had said. The his mind backtracked, registered the words, and reeled in horror.

"What?" Basil asked.

"You are no longer my heir," Mr. Paisley repeated. "I am not disowning you, Basil. You are still my son, and I will still teach you to work and see that you have some means when I die, but I can no longer entrust my life's work to you, not after this incident. Once we reach a town, I will hire a lawyer to update my will and make your brother my heir."

"Chauncy? He's a child."

"And one day he will be a man. A good man, I believe, a capable man, a man of self-control."

Basil blinked up at him, thinking, *Well, thank you for telling me, Father. Now, I know that I must not allow you to reach a town. I had wanted more, but your current fortune will have to suffice.*

His father frowned at him with annoying disappointment bordering on pity.

In response, Basil dipped his head, pretending shame, and repressed the urge badly to pound his father's skull off the nail keg upon which he was sitting.

But of course, he could not do that now. People outside were setting up the night camp. They had definitely heard Mr. Paisley's angry shouting.

Luckily, he'd lowered his voice when he'd broken the news about the will.

If he'd shouted that, Basil would have been suspected of murder no matter how patiently he waited to kill his father.

As it was, he would need to wait at least a week before he struck. During that time, he would play the mild-mannered son. He would act the part of the young man being crafted by the West. He would even do some work. Anything to please his father and make everything appear well between them.

Then, when the time was right, he would kill the fool.

But first, he had other business to attend to.

"There is darkness in you, Basil, a wild cruelty that knows no bounds. I had hoped the West would make a man of you, but now I fear it has made a monster of you instead."

"I'm so sorry to disappoint you, Father," Basil said, summoning a single tear. "I will try harder. I know it's too late to regain my status as your heir, and I understand your decision, but I am desperate to show you that I can be a good man. Please give me a chance to redeem myself, Father. Again, not as your heir, but as your son."

Mr. Paisley nodded, smiling sadly. "Of course, my son. Of course."

Basil wiped his eye and thanked his father and dipped out of the wagon.

Outside, people stared. They were smart enough not to smile, but too dumb to hide the laughter in their eyes. Mentally, he noted every one of them and added them to the list. Of course, many were already on the list. Those, he underscored as deserving extra attention prior to death.

But that was all for later. Presently, he had more pressing work.

He rounded up his two men, Pearson and Clark, and left the camp, where he couldn't be overheard.

"Get ready to ride," he told them.

The men, who always liked the sort of work he'd hired them to do, smiled.

"What are we gonna do, boss?" Pearson asked.

"While everyone else beds down, we're riding back out to the trail."

"What for?"

"You know what for."

The two men looked suddenly ill at ease.

"You don't mean…" Clark stammered.

"I mean you two are finally going to earn your keep. I didn't hire you to drive wagons."

"How would we even find them?"

"We're leaving now, before we lose the light. We'll tell everyone we're going hunting."

"You think they'll believe us?"

"They're hungry, Pearson. Hungry people are always ready to believe anybody with food. That's the way the world works."

"Yeah, but boss, those people could be anywhere."

Basil shook his head. "Didn't you hear Doc Henderson? The mountain boy and his breed have a place just a couple of miles off the trail. They're bound to leave plenty of sign. So long as we get there before we lose light, we'll have no trouble tracking them back to where they're staying."

Pearson and Clark exchanged infuriatingly cowardly looks. He wouldn't have thought it possible.

"I don't know, boss," Pearson said. "That tall'un's got ice water in his veins."

Clark nodded. "He ain't got an ounce of bluff in him. That might be more trouble than's worth huntin'."

"And that kid with him's cut of the same cloth," Pearson said. "I believe he woulda shot us, I truly do."

Basil shook his head. What a couple of idiots. "None of that is going to do them any good when they're sleeping, is it? We'll sneak over there, wait for them to go nighty night, then shoot them in their bedrolls."

Other men would have recoiled at the suggestion, but Basil knew Pearson and Clark would not. After all, that's why he'd hired them. They were hardened criminals. Sometimes, that's what you need to get things done: a couple of gunmen with no scruples whatsoever.

Clark smiled, showing a jagged set of tobacco-stained teeth. "I thought you meant we was gonna face up to him."

"So'd I," Pearson laughed. "Which sounded like a good way to get killed. But I'll shoot him while he sleeps."

"Excellent," Basil said, hoping in his dark heart that he would catch little Miss Mullen and her big, strong protector making love. It would save him the trouble of stripping her.

CHAPTER 31

After showing the Mullens around the place, enjoying their amazement, and giving all credit to Seeker and his parents, Heck asked Tom and Seeker if they wanted to head downstream and bathe.

Seeker shrugged and said he'd go along.

Tom declined. "I'll stay here and keep an eye on everybody. A bath sounds good, but I'd be changing back into the same dirty clothes."

"Well," Heck said, gathering his own things, along with the soap and Seeker-sized duds he'd traded for with passing emigrants earlier that week, "we'll get you fixed up soon. We'll cart some meat and apples up to the trail. Folks'll trade you the shirts right off their backs."

"I'll come downstream with you, Heck," Hope joked, and Heck felt his face go hot again. She sure knew how to upend his apple cart.

"Hope Marie," her mother scolded through a smile, "that's

enough of that sort of talk. You'll stay here and help me cook these men a good dinner. Oh, but it is nice to be in a kitchen again."

"Ma'am," Heck said, "old Seeker and me aren't the best chefs in the world, but we'd be happy to fix some grub. Y'all must be tired."

"Thank you, Heck," Mrs. Mullen said. "You certainly are a gallant young man, but I was speaking truthfully when I said I was happy to find myself in a kitchen again."

"I'm afraid, ma'am, that you might find ours lacking in certain provisions."

Mrs. Mullen shook her head. "I see flour and apples, meat and molasses, potatoes and salt. I made do with less during the lean years before Mr. Mullen and I purchased our farm. It will be a joy to cook for you again."

Heck made sure that the extra guns were loaded and that the Mullens knew how to use them. Then he and Seeker headed downstream, stripped out of their filthy clothes, and waded into the current.

The day was hot and bright, but snow melt and mountain springs fed the stream. Heck felt like he'd fallen through the ice in December.

"They seem like good folks," Seeker remarked, scrubbing the dirt from his wiry arms.

"They're the best family I ever met," Heck said, and he told again the story of how they had taken him in and helped him to get his start. "They always believed in me. And that made all the difference."

"That's the way I feel about you, Heck."

"What do you mean?"

Seeker shrugged, suddenly sheepish. "I don't know. You believe in me."

"I do."

"Well, I appreciate it."

"And I appreciate you, little brother. I appreciate you taking me in and feeding me. I appreciate you having my back when folks want to kill me. I appreciate you opening your home to the Mullens like you are."

"It ain't my home, Heck. It's ours. Remember? You said we're partners, and partners share everything."

"Thanks, little brother. But you know what I mean. I appreciate you." He grinned. "And I'll appreciate you even more now that you're washing the stink off."

"You're one to talk, Heck. You smelled like a dead skunk."

Heck threw back his head and laughed.

When they finished, they washed their duds, lathering them up and beating them against the rocks, and then dressed in the clean clothes they'd brought along.

Heck wore cotton trousers and the brand new, light blue shirt he'd bought for just this occasion.

"Wow, Heck," Seeker said, "you look like a fancy man."

"A fancy man, huh?" Heck laughed. "Well, don't let looks deceive you, little brother. Under these new duds, I'm still the same old rotten mountain man."

"Hope'll like it," Seeker said.

Heck shrugged.

"She sure is pretty," the boy said.

Heck nodded. "She sure is. And that ain't the half of it. I never met anybody half so full of light in all my life. She is kind and sweet and playful. She loves her family and loves God and loves to laugh. She is a pure delight, little brother."

"Do you love her?"

"With every fiber of my body and soul. But don't go telling anybody."

Seeker looked at him funny. "Why not?"

"Well, little brother, it's complicated. But Hope's had a hard go of it."

"Yeah, she has."

"And that boy I had to knock some sense into, he was lording his position over her, saying she had to be his woman or he'd quit feeding her and kick her daddy out of the wagon."

"I'm glad you busted him up."

"He deserved it, and I was happy to oblige. But what I'm trying to say is, I don't want Hope feeling like she's jumped out of the frying pan and into the fire."

Seeker tilted his head again. "Sometimes, you don't make no sense."

"Stick with me, little brother, and you'll learn a thing or two. See, what I'm trying to say is, I don't want Hope to feel like I expect anything.

"That old boy I put the knuckles to was feeding them and carting her daddy out of the trail. Now, we're feeding them and giving her daddy a place to rest. And I don't want the Mullens thinking I'll kick them out like he did if she doesn't love me back."

Seeker looked at him like he was crazy. "But you'd never do that."

"I know that, and you know that, but I don't want them wondering for a second, so I'm not saying anything for the moment. I'd hate for Hope to say she loved me just because she feared what would happen if she didn't."

Now it was Seeker's turn to throw back his head with laughter. "Heck, you might be older'n me and smarter by a stretch, but you sure don't seem it now. That girl loves you more than she loves to breathe. Anybody can see that!"

CHAPTER 32

"My oh my," Mrs. Mullen said, when they came back through the door, "don't you boys clean up nice? Don't you think so, Hope dear?"

Hope just stood there, staring at Heck and biting her lip. She was red as a radish.

"Hope?"

"Huh? Sorry, Mother. I didn't hear you."

Mrs. Mullen looked back and forth between Heck and her daughter with a knowing smile. "I said, didn't these young men clean up nicely?"

"Oh, yes. Yes, ma'am. Very nicely." She touched a hand to her hair and frowned. "Makes me wish…"

"Well, we can't get cleaned up yet," Mrs. Mullen said. "We're in the middle of making dinner."

"Yes, Mother. I don't have anything clean to change into anyway."

"Like I told Tom," Heck said, "we'll get y'all some more

clothes soon. If folks don't want apples or venison, I got some money squirreled away."

"Well, thank you, Heck. That's very kind of you," Mrs. Mullen said. She smiled for a moment, then nudged her daughter. "Isn't it, Hope?"

Hope, who had been staring dazedly at Heck, shook out of it. "What? Oh, yes, Mother. Very kind." She smiled at Heck. "Thank you, Heck. You sure are handsome."

He smiled, feeling color come into his cheeks as Hope turned bright red again. She slapped a hand over her mouth, and her emerald eyes went huge with disbelief and embarrassment.

Mrs. Mullen grinned at her daughter's discomfort. "Well, Hope, why don't you and Tom take some of this broth in to your father and see if you can get him to take any?"

"Yes, ma'am," Hope said. Still blushing, she spooned some broth into a cup and carried it to the back corner, where they'd fixed a pallet for her father.

When they sat down to a dinner of fresh bread, venison steaks, and wild onion and potato soup, Hope asked who was going to pray.

Mrs. Mullen turned to Heck, who sat in his usual spot at the head of the table. Hope sat on his right. Mrs. Mullen was to his left. Seeker sat at the far end, and between the boy and Mrs. Mullen sat Tom.

"That job falls to the man of the house," Mrs. Mullen said, nodding to Heck.

"Oh," Heck said and put down the spoon he'd been about to plunge into the soup, the smell of which was so rich and good, he'd nearly forgotten his manners.

He'd never spent much time in the company of women, and he knew his manners had been rough enough before disappearing for two years into the wilderness with good old Rabbit Foot. He'd have to be on his toes over the coming days if he wanted to avoid embarrassing himself.

He cleared his throat, not knowing exactly what to say. It had been a long time since he'd even heard someone say grace. Finally, he just spoke the truth.

"Lord, I thank you so much for the people around this table and for Mr. Mullen over yonder. Thank you for bringing us together and for putting food on this table. Please help this meal to nourish us, and please, Lord, lay your healing hand upon Mr. Mullen and bring him back to us. In Jesus' precious name we pray. Amen."

"Amen," everybody chorused, and they fell to eating.

It was all Heck could do not to moan at how good the soup tasted, and the fresh bread was even better. Even the venison, which he ate frequently, was delicious.

"Ma'am, this here is the best darn grub I ever et!" Seeker declared as only the excited son of a true mountain man could put it.

For as wonderful as the food was, however, the conversation was even better. It sure was good to be reunited with these people.

Heck had missed Mrs. Mullen's kindness and soft-spoken wisdom; Tom's big-spirited friendliness and excitement; and every last thing about Hope.

It was all he could do to keep his eyes off her, and Heck reckoned he could happily spend eternity staring at the girl's face as she ate, talked, and laughed. With every passing second, she grew more lovely to him.

After dinner, they checked on Mr. Mullen again. He was sleeping peacefully, and his fever seemed better.

Tom asked Seeker to show him the secret passageway he'd hidden in for so long, and the pair headed back into the mountain.

While the women cleaned up dinner, Heck grabbed his rifle and went outside to see to the horses and check on how they were getting along.

The cool of evening was upon the land, shadows were deepening in the canyon, and an owl hooted from the pines.

Heck paused outside, swept his gaze across the little garden, then turned and took in the cabin and corral.

Suddenly, he possessed unbelievable wealth. That had nothing to do with his $15,000 and everything to do with this little setup and the wonderful people indoors. All the money in the world couldn't have given him a whisker of happiness up against the joy he felt, knowing the Mullens and Seeker were inside.

It doesn't take much for a man to be happy, not if he has his head screwed on tight. Food, family, a roof over his head, a plot of ground to call his own, a bit of work, and two strong hands to do it with.

He had all that, and he was head over heels in love besides.

Did Hope feel the same way?

She sure seemed happy to see him, but that didn't mean she loved him.

It didn't seem possible that such a wonderful young woman

could even be interested in a rough-and-ready young man like himself.

But his mind whipped back to the sun-dappled day three years earlier, when Hope had stopped him on the road and asked him to kiss her.

His heart quickened. She was inside. The girl he had kissed, the girl he had dreamed of all these years, was just inside the house.

He wanted to march in there and take her in his arms and tell her he loved her and kiss her and kiss her and kiss her.

But that would ruin everything. Mrs. Mullen would crown him with a frying pan, for starters, but beyond that, what if Hope resisted his attentions?

No matter how much he wanted to wrap her up in an embrace and confess his feelings, he had to take his time. Especially because he didn't want her to feel uncomfortable.

Yes, he wanted her to love him, wanted it more than anything in the whole world, but he didn't want to force that love, didn't want her to say the words unless they were true, didn't want her to fear any consequences of not loving him, and didn't want her pledging herself to him for any reason other than love.

Which is why he also decided not to mention the fortune he had amassed. Not that Hope would feign love for money. But after dealing with Basil, she might be traumatized. She might, fearing for her family, convince herself of certain things if doing so meant her family would be safe and secure forever.

Which they would be, so long as they allowed Heck to help them, and he would do that no matter how Hope felt.

But she didn't know that.

Also, Hope was holding up well despite her circumstances, but with Mr. Mullen's health hanging in the balance, Heck wouldn't feel right, springing the whole subject on her.

So he ambled out to the corral and called out to Red, where the stallion was showing off for the two mares... including Hope's Dolly.

Tom's horse had joined the other geldings at the opposite side of the corral.

Heck took care of the horses. When he came back out, the cabin door swung open, and his heart set to bucking.

Here came Hope, walking toward him with a smile on her face, the last light of dying day setting her auburn hair afire.

"Are you hiding out here?" she asked.

"Not hardly," he said, leaning up against the corral. "Just finished taking care of the horses. I gotta warn you. Looks like Red has designs on Dolly."

Hope came up to the fence beside him, propped one boot on the lower rail, then folded her forearms on the top rail and rested her chin there, staring across the corral at her prancing mare, who was clearly encouraging the big stallion's attentions.

"Well, he'd best look out," she said, "because it seems to me that Dolly has designs on him, too. Who could blame her? He's big and strong and knows what he wants."

She turned her lovely face to him then, her green eyes luminous in the mellow evening light. "Do you know what you want, Heck?"

His heart leapt at the question. Did she mean what he thought she meant?

He nodded. "I know what I want."

"Good," she said, turning again to face the horses, "because I know what I want, too. I told myself not to say anything, but as you might have noticed, I sometimes talk when I shouldn't. Heck, I'm just going to tell you—"

"Hope," he said, seizing her by the shoulders and turning her gently toward him, "I still love you. I never stopped loving you."

And just like that, despite all his planning and best intentions, he had confessed everything.

Now, his face burned, and his heart hammered, as the gorgeous young woman stared up at him… and smiled.

"You have no idea how happy that makes me, Heck. No idea at all. I love you so very much. I never stopped loving you, either. I never stopped thinking about you. Ever since the moment we met, I loved you, and it has grown stronger day by day."

He hauled her close and lowered his mouth, and suddenly, they were kissing again, frantically, feverishly, both of them having dreamed daily of this moment for years.

Finally, Hope broke the kiss and stepped back, panting with desire, her eyes wild with passion. She smiled but shook her head. "If Mother comes out here and catches us, she'll tan my hide."

He nodded, wanting to grab hold of Hope and keep kissing her, but he reined in hard and nodded his head. "All right, Hope. I sure did like that, though."

"So did I. Say it again, Heck."

"I love you with all my heart, Hope Mullen."

"And I love you with all my heart, Heck Martin."

They stood there, smiling at each other, both of them deliriously happy.

Then Hope's face grew serious. "Heck, do you still want to… I mean, do you love me enough to—"

"Wait," Heck said sharply, cutting her off.

Because suddenly, Burly was stomping and blowing and staring into the trees behind the cabin.

CHAPTER 33

Heck picked up his rifle and stepped in front of Hope.

His eyes scanned the gloom. He lifted his nose and sniffed the air.

"What are you doing, Heck?"

"We got trouble," he whispered. "I would've smelled them sooner if I wasn't so wrapped up in you."

"Huh? Smelled them? Smelled who? What's going on, Heck?"

"Come on, let's get you inside. Act natural in case they're watching."

"Watching? You're scaring me, Heck," she said, but he was pleased that despite her fear, she kept her voice low and did indeed act natural as they slipped between the fence rails, crossed the corral, and entered the stable. "Who's watching us? Is it Indians?"

"No, they smell like white men."

"I'm confused, Heck."

"You live out in the mountains, you come to rely on your sense of smell. I can smell their soap and camp smoke and their dinner."

He pointed to the back of the space, where the stone corridor led back to the cabin. "Just keep making rights until you see everybody, okay?"

"Okay."

"Tell Seeker and Tom that Basil and his boys are here. Tell them to sit tight and wait till they hear gunfire, all right?"

"All right. But wait, Heck—where are you going?"

"I'm going back out there to turn the tables on them. I'm not sure how close they are. If they haven't seen us yet, I should be able to give them a little surprise."

"Give me your pistol. I'll come with you."

Heck shook his head. "I gotta do this alone."

She didn't argue. "Okay, Heck." Then she grabbed him by the shirt front and pulled him to her and kissed him deeply. "You be careful out there. If you get yourself killed, I'm going to be mad at you."

He grinned at that, kissed her again, and slipped back into the gathering darkness. Staying low, he stuck to the face of the cliff, dipped out between the fence rails, and sniffed the air again.

There. They were somewhere off to the right, likely in that jutting arm of trees just beyond the cabin. Which made sense, given that they would've come down from the trail.

He climbed the slope, moving quietly, calling upon all those many months of experience in the wilderness. Following a game trail, he worked his way through the trees and across the slope, passing behind the cabin, keeping his eyes wide open, and pausing from time to time to strain his ears.

There... he could hear their voices.

Just as he had expected, they were positioned in the trees just north of the cabin.

Moving with upmost care, he slipped as silently as a cougar through the gloomy forest until he tucked in behind a flat-topped boulder just uphill from them. He could see them down there, no more than seventy yards away.

It was Basil, all right. He had the other two men, the pair Heck had backed down, with him.

All three men carried rifles or shotguns. Probably shotguns. Because Heck was certain now what these snakes were planning to do.

They were waiting for Heck and the others to go to sleep. Then they planned to sneak up to the cabin and shoot the men while they slept. Probably the women, too. Though knowing what little he knew of Basil, he figured the brute would have other plans for Hope before shooting her.

The old killing frost settled over Heck as he got down on his belly and crawled silently forward.

He drew within forty yards and slipped his barrel over a fallen log. It was almost dark now, but their position was better lit than his, and Heck had great night vision, so he had no trouble making them out or hearing their voices.

He shouldered the Hawken and adjusted his position but held fire, allowing them to convict themselves.

Had he had any doubts, what he heard would have burned them to a crisp.

"Shoot him first," Basil said.

"All three of us?"

"Yes. We're not taking any chances with him. Then we'll shoot the rest of them."

"The women, too?" one of Basil's thugs asked.

"Yes, but not right away. First, just kill the men and the little breed. I'm going to have my way with Hope before I kill her."

"Can I have the mom?" one of the others asked.

"Sure, Clark. Do whatever you want with her. Just don't go getting attached. You have to kill her when we're finished. Same goes for Hope. You can both have a turn after I'm through with her. We'll show her what she's good for. Then we'll kill her, too."

Listening, Heck burned with rage.

"Pretty cold work, boss," one of the men remarked.

"You're not turning yellow on me, are you, Pearson? I seem to remember when I bought your freedom from the gallows that you were going to hang for rape and murder."

"I was. And no, I'm not turning yeller. I was just saying was all. Cold work. I was surprised to hear you suggest it was all. I mean, you got breeding and money."

"No one gets rich without doing cold work along the way."

Heck had heard enough. He pulled his pistol and checked it and laid it on the ground beside him, then did the same with his tomahawk.

Then he got behind his rifle again, put the sights on the thug to Basil's right, set the trigger, and waited for the other hired gun to lean forward.

When he did, Heck pulled the trigger. A second later, he was on his feet, pistol in one hand, tomahawk in the other.

Both gunmen were down. The big .54 caliber round had blown through one man and then the other.

Basil gave a squeal and fired his weapon by accident. Then, seeing Heck charging, he gave a cry of terror, threw down his rifle, and tugged at the pistol shoved through his belt.

Heck fired, nailing him in the pelvis, pulled back the hammer, and fired again, catching him through the guts as he dropped. Basil hitched around on the ground, making a weird, guttural noise like a gut-shot elk.

Heck drew back his arm, ready to hurl the tomahawk.

Seeing him, Basil squawked with terror and tossed his gun aside. "Money," he whined. "So much money. All yours. Just... have mercy."

"I'll show the same mercy you were going to show my family," Heck said and let the tomahawk fly, a thing he'd done countless times in the Rockies.

The slender axe whirled, tumbling through the air, and slammed to an abrupt stop, making a hollow *thock* as it sunk like a wedge into Basil's forehead, splitting his skull and killing him instantly.

It was better than he deserved.

But while Heck had a thing or two to learn about table manners, he reckoned he knew a thing or two more than the Mullens about such grisly matters.

By killing this mad dog outright, he'd not only fulfilled his promise to do just that and protected his people but had also spared Hope and the others the pain and confusion of what to do with a gut-shot villain.

"Heck!" Tom yelled, charging up the hill. "Where are you?"

Seeker, sounding calmer, called, "You kill all of them, big brother?"

Heck grinned in the darkness. Yeah, that boy would do to ride the river with. "That's right, little brother. Killed them all. We got nothing to worry about."

CHAPTER 34

Hope wept.

She wept with gratitude and relief to know Heck was okay, and she wept with fear and revulsion because three men she had known now laid dead upon the slope behind the cabin.

Or at least they had. Heck, Tom, and Seeker were out there in the night, moving the bodies. Where, she did not know. She didn't even want to know.

Nothing felt quite real.

Not long ago, Hope had led a happy if wistful life on a farm in Kentucky. That's what she wanted again, more than anything, a nice, calm life on a farm somewhere.

But at the moment, that didn't seem possible.

Because this was a land of violence, and you never knew what the next hour might bring. Any single day could yank a body back and forth between joy and despair over and over.

So much violence, so much death.

The bandits, the fight on the trail, now this.

Basil was dead. Pearson and Clark were dead.

They were bad men. They brought it on themselves.

But they were still dead, and it was hard to fully comprehend.

Why, just this morning, Basil had bowed to her and given her the phony smile and threatened to—

Yes, he deserved his death. And she had no illusions about why he had come here, what he would have done to all of them, not just her but Mother and Daddy, Tom and Heck, Seeker…

Yes, he had earned this fate.

But still she wept because she felt so much emotion.

Not just revulsion and confusion over the killing. Also the joy of finding Heck and the relief of coming to this place. Atop that, she worried about so many other things: Daddy's condition, starvation, Indians, wild animals.

And she was dirty. So dirty. With no clean clothes and nothing else of her own, except Dolly. She'd lost everything. Her family had lost everything.

Earlier, the joy of being reunited with Heck had washed away her worries. She loved him so much, and it was the thrill of her life to hear him say he still loved her, that he had never stopped loving her.

But then Basil and his men had come, and Heck had gone off into the night, and the gunfire had erupted, and she had been so scared, so very scared, and then so relieved when she'd heard Heck was okay, but now, it felt like everything was whirling, and she couldn't stop crying, couldn't catch her breath—

"Hope Marie Mullen," Mother said sternly, seizing her by the shoulders. "Stop crying this instant."

"I... can't..."

Mother squeezed her shoulders and stared hard into her eyes. "You can and you will. You must."

Hope nodded and wiped her eyes, but the sobs kept coming.

"Take a deep breath," Mother said, still gripping her shoulders.

Hope tried, got halfway, and let it out with another convulsion of emotion.

"Again."

Hope tried and did a little better.

Mother handed her a hankie. "Blow your nose, dear. That's it. Breathe. That's better."

Mother's voice grew softer as Hope gained control, little by little.

Once the tears had stopped, Mother's voice was as soft and comforting as a baby's blanket. But despite their softness, her words spoke only the hard truth.

"Hope, I want no more tears from you. You must be strong for Heck. He is a good man, a strong man, the sort of man who can survive in this brutal land. It was a hard thing he did out there, just as it was a hard thing he did, dispensing with the bandits who shot your father. Not to mention the way he faced up to Basil and his men back on the trail."

Hope nodded, holding in the tears and focusing on her breathing. "I know, Mother, and I appreciate him. It's just—"

"You've had a hard time of it, dear, and I'm very proud of the way you've handled yourself. If I know you half as well as I think I know you, you've been bottling up all your worries, and the shooting tonight popped the cork and let them all out at once."

Hope nodded but didn't trust herself to speak, as her mother's understanding triggered another wave of emotion in her.

"I don't mean to sound harsh, Hope, but you're going to have to shove that stopper in place again. If you must cry, wait until you know Heck won't hear you. Do you understand?"

Hope nodded, knowing her mother was right. "I'm sorry, Mother."

"Sorry? What on Earth for? For being human? For having feelings? For being a wonderful young woman who loves her family and, if I'm not mistaken, loves a certain young man who will be returning to the cabin soon?"

Hope sniffed and smiled sheepishly. "I do, Mother. I really do love Heck."

"I can see why. He's a fine young man. I will pray for you both."

"Thank you, Mother."

"You are welcome, my dear. But in the meantime, you must be strong. The strength of men and women is different. Men go forth and face danger head on. They put themselves between us and danger, risk their lives to keep us safe, ruin their bodies to provide nourishment and shelter for ours. At least, that's what good men do. And Heck is a good man. He's shown his strength and compassion since we first met him."

"He is very strong. I could never be that strong."

"That's where you're wrong, Hope. You are very strong, too. And if you're going to pursue a life with Heck, you will need to be as strong as he is."

"As strong as Heck? But that's not—"

"Yes, as strong as Heck. Perhaps even stronger. You'll need to be."

"But, I can't—"

"Listen, Hope. As I was saying, the strength of women is different than the strength of men. We're different creatures, praise God, with different bodies, different minds, and different burdens to carry."

"Like childbirth?"

"Yes, a woman shows her strength in childbirth, but she also shows her strength in raising those children the best she can while keeping the family together. That means a lot of things. It means hard work that often goes unnoticed and patience that is often taken for granted. It means knowing her husband. His moods, his needs, how to please him, how to talk to him while allowing him to remain who he is, the strong man she needs him to be.

"But a woman's strength is far more than that. It allows us to meet the constant demands of the life of a wife and mother. Like men, we work hard and bear up under heat and cold, hunger and thirst. But our strength is quieter than the strength of men.

"Men show their strength by killing bears and fighting Indians. You can feel their strength in their hands, see it in their jaws and muscles, hear it in the words their deep voices speak. And that is as God intended it."

Hope nodded, picturing all those qualities in Heck.

"But much of our strength comes down to nights like tonight. We will show our strength by not crying in front of Heck. He doesn't want tears. So we will not cry in front of him. We smile and thank him and feed him and pray with and for him, even if it takes every ounce of strength to hold in our emotions. Do you understand?"

"Yes, Mother."

"Good. Because that is the burden of a wife and a mother. We must put family first, always, and give them what they need. Usually, our efforts go unnoticed, but that is okay. Ours is a secret strength, and—"

The door swung open, and Heck, apparently finished with his gruesome work, came inside, followed by Tom and Seeker.

Instantly, Heck noticed Hope's puffy eyes, and his face filled with concern. "Are you okay, Hope?"

"Yes, Heck, I am okay. I'm just so thankful that we're here with you, and that you did what you did to protect us and that we can count on you to keep us safe."

And even though Hope had struggled to stop crying, speaking these words made her feel better. Because they were the truth—she knew that now, seeing it clearly—and speaking the truth had brushed away the confusion and set her free from her whirling thoughts and worries.

CHAPTER 35

The next morning, Heck woke early and went out into the stillness. Seeker followed, as silent as a bobcat on damp grass. The air held a pleasant chill, and high above, stars yet twinkled in the darkness.

His body wanted coffee, but the Mullens were still sleeping. Which made sense. They'd been through a lot.

Besides, not everyone woke in darkness to start his day.

But like his father, Heck had always been an early riser. There was something in him, a thing as restless as a starving wolf, a force that drove him ever onward.

Today, he would hunt fresh meat or catch some fish. Then, he would begin work on another cabin. He had some ideas about its size and shape and how to keep it as defensible as possible, but he would talk with the Mullens before committing to anything.

With Tom's knack for leatherwork, he might have some

good ideas. Hope and her mother were both intelligent, and they might have some good thoughts, too.

He sure did wish Mr. Mullen, who'd probably built plenty of cabins, was awake.

He explained all this to Seeker, who nodded.

"Your daddy sure did pick a good spot here," Heck said. "From what I've seen of this territory, there's no other valley quite like this one. You have timber and grass and game, rich soil and running water chock full of trout, those caves. It's like God Himself gave you this amazing gift."

"Gave *us* this amazing gift, you mean, big brother," Seeker said.

Heck nodded at that.

"Will the Mullens stay with us, do you think?"

Heck nodded. "Through winter, anyway. After that, I'm not sure where they'll want to be."

Seeker kicked a pebble with his moccasin. "Will you go with them?"

"I'd like to. And I'm hoping you'll come with me, little brother."

Seeker's grin flashed in the low light. "I'd like that. We're partners, right?"

"Partners." Heck held out his hand.

Seeker shook it firmly, looking him in the eyes.

They sat in silence for a long moment. Off to the east, stars faded into the graying sky with the dim light of approaching sunrise.

Now was the time to hunt or fish, but apparently, Seeker still had more to say.

"Heck?"

"Yeah?"

"You gonna ask her?"

"Huh?"

"Hope. You gonna ask her?"

"Ask her what?"

"You know, to marry you."

Staring out into the coming day, Heck nodded. "Yeah, I reckon I will."

"Good. That's good."

"But I gotta do something first."

"What's that?"

"Just something I gotta do. If I can."

"Oh."

They were silent for a time. As the sun rose, the canyon filled with birdsong.

"Heck?"

"Yeah?"

"If you ask Hope and she says yes and you get married, can I still come with you?"

"Of course, little brother. You're stuck with me for life."

Seeker bobbed his head up and down, grinning from ear to ear. "All right, then." He stood. "I reckon I'll go catch some trout."

Laughing, Heck stood, too. "Hold up there, partner, and let the master show you how it's done."

THAT DAY, WITH THE HELP OF TOM AND SEEKER, HECK LAID OUT the cabin site and drew up some plans.

He'd helped build cabins as a boy, and he and Rabbit Foot had built a cabin for their winter camp.

As he was working out these plans, Seeker gave him some great news.

"Follow me," the boy said and led Heck downstream a short way, then turned into a dim gully that hugged the curve of the mountain.

"There," Seeker said, pointing.

"Little brother, you just made me a very happy man."

"Pa cut those two years back to let them dry. Figured it'd come in handy."

"Your pa was a smart man," Heck said. "And I'm much obliged. I reckon we have enough to build a cabin right here."

"If not, there's more downstream a ways."

"A very smart man, indeed. We'll learn from him and cut more timber after we clear these, get it drying for next year."

They went back to the stable and fetched Seeker's dad's drag harness, hitched up Burly and one of the geldings, and set to work hauling the timber back to their clearing.

On the fourth or fifth return trip, Hope came running out of the cabin with tears streaming down her pretty face.

Heck rushed to her. "What's wrong, Hope?"

"Come quick, Heck," Hope sobbed. "It's Daddy!"

CHAPTER 36

Mr. Mullen sat up on his pallet, holding a mug of steaming broth in one hand. The other hand poked gingerly at the wound on his temple. "Feel like I went fifty rounds with old Bendigo Thompson himself, but yeah, I'm back, praise the good Lord."

Seeing Heck, Mr. Mullen beamed. "Well, look what the cat dragged in. They said you was here, my boy, but I didn't believe them. Chalked it up to fever dreams, I did. How are you, Heck?"

"I'm awful happy to see you up, sir," Heck said, walking over and holding out his hand.

"A handshake? Oh, you do wound my heart, Heck. Three years, and that's what you're gonna give your old friend Tom Mullen? A handshake? Get down here and give me a hug, you great bearded lug."

Laughing, Heck knelt and wrapped the man in an embrace, careful not to hurt him.

Mr. Mullen held tightly to him. "Oh, Heck, how I've longed to see you, son. Sounds like you've had quite a time."

"I'm just happy to see everyone again."

Mr. Mullen leaned back and held Heck at arm's length. "Look at you, boy. Just look at you. Fearsome, that's what you are. How I'd hate to see you standing across the ring from me. Oh, but we have much to talk over. You must tell me of every round of every fight, especially the match with Mitchell." Mr. Mullen clapped him on the shoulder. "The heavyweight champion of the West. Oh, they'd be just a quaking in their boots if you went back to the ring now, Heck."

Mr. Mullen laughed at the thought then winced and rubbed his head.

"Please, dear, do take it easy," Mrs. Mullen said, touching her husband's arm. "There will be plenty of time for catching up with Heck after you've rested and had more broth."

"Aye, you're right, love. It's just so good to see Heck again."

"Actually, ma'am," Heck said, "would you mind if I spoke with Mr. Mullen for just a moment longer? It won't take but a minute."

Mrs. Mullen smiled and nodded, a knowing twinkle in her eye. "Certainly, Heck. Would you prefer to speak with Mr. Mullen alone?"

"Yes, ma'am."

Seeker took his cue and left the cabin. Tom and Hope looked confused, but Mrs. Mullen herded them outside.

"Heck," Mr. Mullen said, "before you have your say, I just want to thank you. Man to man. From what Mrs. Mullen and the children tell me, you saved my life and theirs as well, along with Hope's virtue, all while I was laid out cold. You did what I couldn't do, son, and you saved the people I love. D'ya know what that means to a man?"

Heck shrugged. "I'm glad I was able to help, sir."

"Ah, Heck, you're one in a million, boy, one in a million. And look at you. What a man you've become. Look at those hands. What've you been living on, whiskey and gunpowder?"

"Mostly meat, sir."

"Ha! It shows."

"And enough lard that I shed water when it rains."

That made Mr. Mullen laugh—at least until he winced again. "Well, what is it you wanted to say, my boy? I know Mrs. Mullen is terribly worried for me. I'd hate for her to come back in here and drive you out before you'd had your say."

"Well, sir, it's like this," Heck started, and he gave it to him straight, explaining how he felt and what he thought, and wrapped up with what seemed to him the most important question in the world.

Mr. Mullen blinked at him for a second.

Then a huge grin spread across the man's face, and he seized Heck's hand in both of his and pumped it up and down with such strength that it would seem he'd never even been injured. "Yes, Heck. Yes, a thousand times over. Oh, my boy, you have no idea how my heart sings at the prospect. Nothing in the whole wide world would make me happier!"

CHAPTER 37

"Where are we going, Heck?" Hope asked, following him up the steep game trail.

"You'll see," he said, holding onto her hand in case she slipped.

"So mysterious," she laughed. "But it's okay. As long as I'm with you, I'm happy."

"I feel the same way, Hope," he said.

What he also felt was a little nervous. Which made little sense, considering everything he'd gone through in life, but emotions are curious things. After all, many of the world's toughest men end up wrapped tightly around the little fingers of their baby daughters.

"I'm so happy, Heck," Hope said. "I just can't tell you how happy I am. I'd been miserable and worried for so long. Frightened, too. Terribly frightened."

"Well, you don't have to be frightened anymore."

She gave his hand a squeeze. "I know, Heck. As long as I'm with you, I know I have nothing to fear."

Of course, Heck knew they would have plenty of concerns in this territory. They would have to keep an eye out for bandits, desperate folks coming off the trail, wayward prospectors, and most of all, Indians.

This was Shoshone country, and most folks got along with the Shoshone, but the Cheyenne, Arapaho, Sioux, Crow, and Blackfeet rode these trails, too, especially during spring raiding or times of war.

But those were his concerns, not hers, and he would do everything in his power to protect her from any threat.

"But everything is wonderful now," Hope went on.

She was different today. More energetic, happier, quick to smile and laugh... more like the girl he'd first fallen in love with three years earlier. It warmed his heart to see her coming fully to life again.

"I'm reunited with you," she said, "and Daddy is awake again. I'm so happy, I could burst."

"I'm glad you're happy, Hope. I'm happy, too. But don't go bursting or you'll miss the view."

They topped the ridge and stood beside a tumble of boulders clustered at the base of the final peak, which rose high above them in a jagged saw blade of raw stone. Here and there across that stony peak, solitary cedars squatted, stubborn-looking, stunted, and stocky.

Behind them, everything tumbled away into their valley. It looked small from up here, the stream a thin line that glistened like a vein of precious ore.

"I can't even see our cabin," Hope remarked.

"That's a good thing," Heck said, "and so is this." He pointed to a nearby cluster of boulders.

Hope tilted her head and studied the boulders, still holding his hand though they had topped the rise. "I don't get it. What's good? Wait—is that… steam?"

Heck shook his head. "Smoke."

Hope's eyes widened. "This isn't a volcano, is it? I've heard about them."

"No," Heck laughed. "What you're looking at is our chimney."

"Our chimney? All the way up here?"

"Yup. That's why the smoke's so pale and busted up. Badger was a crafty old mountain man. He vented the fireplace and oven into a chamber with a cracked ceiling, so the smoke drifts up through a series of natural cuts and splits and comes out all the way up here."

"That sure was smart," Hope said.

"It was."

"We owe him a lot."

"We do," he said, tugging her across the boulders toward what he really wanted to show her. "But that's the nature of life. We're always benefiting from those who came before us. Learning their ways, using their tools, and passing it all along to the next generation. Now, right ahead here is what I brought you up here to see."

They passed between two boulders, and the world opened up in a high meadow, where acres and acres and acres of hip-high hay swayed in the breeze.

"Oh, Heck, it's beautiful. What a magical place. Is that hay?"

"It is. Badger worked this meadow. He had planned on selling feed to passing emigrants. I reckon it was a good plan."

Hope nodded. "Very. While we were on the trail, we lost an awful lot of time looking for forage."

"And folks are ready to trade their shot and powder for a sack of apples."

"But it doesn't make any sense, Heck. Our valley, this place, they're so different from the rest of this territory."

Heck spread his hands. "If God smiles on us, who are we to question His generosity?"

Hope nodded. "That is the truth if I've ever heard the truth spoken, Heck. You could make a good living here. A good life, I mean."

"Yes, we could."

"We?" Hope turned her head, looking both excited and frightened.

"Yes, we," Heck said. "I'm not gonna lie. There's a lot of work to be done here. An awful lot. But I grew up tilling mountain soil and planting corn, and I've never minded hard work. And unless I miss my mark, you don't mind it much, either."

"No, sir," Hope said, her voice suddenly soft, almost faint. "I've never minded hard work in the least."

"I love you, Hope. I want to live here with you and your folks and Tom and Seeker. I want to build a life here."

Hope nodded, smiling and biting her lip and looking like she was doing her best to hold back tears.

Heck took a knee before her.

"What I'm trying to say is, Hope Mullen, will you marry me and make me the happiest man in creation?"

"Yes!" Hope said, leaning down and throwing her arms

around his neck and squeezing him tight. "Yes, Heck, yes, I would love to marry you!"

They hugged each other for a long moment, Hope crying and professing her love, Heck echoing her sentiments, until his mouth found hers and they kissed long and passionately, drunk on love and joy.

Finally, Heck took her hand in his. "This afternoon, I'll head up to the trail and try to get a nice dress for you and clothes for your family. And anything else you need. See, now that you're gonna be my wife, I'll let you in on a secret."

"What's that?"

"We're rich."

"Rich?"

He nodded. "From boxing and trapping, I have around fifteen thousand dollars."

Hope's mouth dropped wide open. "Fifteen thousand dollars? Is that even possible?"

Heck laughed. "It's more than possible. It's ours."

Hope popped onto her tiptoes and kissed him again. "I'd marry you if you didn't have two pennies to rub together, Heck, but this news makes me so happy. It makes me feel safe."

"Good," Heck said, loving her smile. "Then, once your daddy's well enough, we'll head up to the trail again. Most of the wagon trains have at least one preacher aboard. We'll get married then and there."

"Oh, Heck, it's a dream come true. I couldn't be happier."

"Same here, Hope. I can't imagine a happier moment. Now, I've been carting something around since I left the mountains back in Kentucky."

He reached into his shirt and yanked the leather string from around his neck then unthreaded the simple golden band from the string upon which he'd carried it all these years. "This is my last link to family, my dear old Mama's wedding ring. I sure would be honored if you would wear it."

Hope's mouth dropped open. "That is the sweetest thing I've ever heard, Heck. But do you really think it would fit?"

"There's one way to find out," Heck said, holding her hand as he slid the golden band onto her ring finger.

"Oh, Heck, it's a miracle," Hope said, holding up the ring and smiling at it through happy tears. "It's a perfect fit."

They kissed again, and he held her tight, looking over her shoulder out at the bright green field, and all the hay he had to cut and carry.

Much work waited for them all, he knew.

They needed to see their crops through to harvest and needed to put up a good deal of hay, wood, and meat if they wanted to survive the winter. There were buildings to build, defenses to erect, folks to meet, countless things to learn, and a lot of surrounding country to explore. He would need to deal with Indians—hopefully on friendly terms—establish a trading business, and eventually hit the trail again in order to fetch things they would be needing, like leatherworking gear for Tom, livestock, and a sturdy wagon or two.

Heck welcomed it all, every last moment, every last bit of work. Because with Hope at his side, nothing could stop him.

He had traveled the whole country. He had fought grown men and ventured city streets, explored river bottoms and haunted the high lonesome, and faced Indians and highwaymen, cougars and bears, heat and cold, living more in the space of three years than most men might live in a lifetime, or even ten lifetimes, but despite all that traveling and searching, only now, only here in this moment, had he finally discovered what he was looking for, a woman who was to him all the things he'd been wanting: family, love, home... and, yes, hope.

THANK YOU FOR READING *HECK'S JOURNEY*.

Heck and Hope's adventures continue in *Heck's Valley*.

If you enjoyed this story, please be a friend and leave a review. When you leave even a short review, you just bought my family dinner, because Amazon will show the book to more people. I sure would appreciate your help.

If you enjoyed the book but don't have time to review, please consider leaving a 5-star rating. It's quick and simple and really helps.

If you'd like to hear about new releases and special sales, join my reader list.

Once more, thanks for reading. I hope our paths cross again.

Until then, don't approach a bull from the front, a horse from the rear, or a fool from any direction.

ABOUT THE AUTHOR

I was born six months before man landed on the moon and lucky enough to grow up in the country, where my family lived largely off the land.

When I wasn't fishing, exploring the woods, or weeding the garden, I devoured comic books like *Two-Gun Kid* and *The Rawhide Kid* before moving on to the exciting adventure stories of Jack London and Louis L'Amour.

Our black-and-white TV only got three channels, though you could lose one and pick up another if you went outside and messed with the antenna. On its grainy screen, we watched *Gunsmoke, Bonanza,* and movies starring John Wayne and Clint Eastwood.

Now a husband and father, I love traveling the West and reading history and fiction alike. My favorite authors are Louis L'Amour, Elmore Leonard, C.J. Petit, and R.O. Lane.

As a writer, I hope to entertain you with fun stories of the old West. My good guys are good, my bad guys are bad, and you'll always find a touch of romance to sweeten the grit.

If you'd like to keep in touch, join my newsletter HERE.

ALSO BY JOHN DEACON

A Man Called Justice (Silent Justice #1)

Justice Returns (Silent Justice #2)

Final Justice (Silent Justice #3)

Justice Rides Again (Silent Justice #4)

Destitution

Heck's Journey (Heck & Hope #1)

Heck's Valley (Heck & Hope #2)

Heck's Gold (Heck & Hope #3)

Heck's Gamble (Heck & Hope #4)

Heck's Stand (Heck & Hope #5)

Printed in Great Britain
by Amazon

21471684R00130